WORKING
MEN

Also by Michael Dorris

Henry Holt and Company
New York

WORKING MEN

STORIES

Michael Dorris

Henry Holt and Company, Inc.
Publishers since 1866
115 West 18th Street
New York, New York 10011

Henry Holt® is a registered
trademark of Henry Holt and Company, Inc.

Published in Canada by Fitzhenry & Whiteside Ltd.,
195 Allstate Parkway, Markham, Ontario L3R 4T8.

Library of Congress Cataloging-in-Publication Data
Dorris, Michael.
Working men: stories/Michael Dorris.—1st ed.
p.   cm.
I. Title.
PS3554.0695W67   1993
813'.54—dc20   93-25558
                                                  CIP

ISBN 0-8050-2296-1

Henry Holt books are available for special promotions and premiums.
For details contact: Director, Special Markets.

First Edition—1993

DESIGNED BY LUCY ALBANESE

Printed in the United States of America
All first editions are printed on acid-free paper.∞

3   5   7   9   10   8   6   4   2

Some of these stories have been published elsewhere: "The Dark Snake" appeared in *The Georgia Review*; "The Benchmark" in *Mother Jones*; "Name Games" in Pen Syndicated Fiction; "Decoration Day" in *The American Voice*; "Earnest Money" and "Shining Agate" in *Ploughshares*; "The Vase" in *Mississippi Valley Review*; "Groom Service" in *Louder Than Words*; "Qiana" in *Glimmer Train*; and "*Oui*" in *Northwest Review*; "Layaway," chosen as the Best Short Story of 1992 by the *Boston Review,* appeared in their October 1993 issue.

Grateful acknowledgment is made to Columbia Pictures Publications for rights to reprint portions of "The Name Game" by Lincoln Chase and Shirley Elliston, © 1964 by Al Galico Music Corp. All rights reserved. Used by permission.

These characters and situations are fictional.

Special thanks for ideas, inspirations, and encouragements to Mary Besy Dorris, Marion Burkhardt, Virginia Burkhardt, Ralph Erdrich, Doug Foster, the late Bill Coughlin, Joe Rogers, the late Hank Greavey, Sandi Campbell, Charles Rembar, and my editor, Marian Wood.

FOR LOUISE

The sifter, the sander
The ear, the eye
The careful heart

CONTENTS

WORKING MEN

THE
BENCHMARK

THE NAKED EYE DECEIVES, that's the first lesson of making a pond. Sea level doesn't matter, is the second. Seek a constant or else you'll misjudge altitude.

To start a job, you drive a nail into a peak of ledge, pound it deep, make it your benchmark, your one-hundred scale. The transit measures from that arbitrary point as you compute all distance in links and chains. Weather patterns can alter, crops grow, houses get built and collapse, but you can return in fifty years and position a tripod, rotate the dials of the spirit until the air bubble precisely crosses the hairline, then aim an alidade at that solitary, centering nail and be in business.

I design a pond to order, I tell property owners as I set up, no two the same. You get more from me than a hole in the earth. There lacks a T square in nature's plan, and I don't pack one in my back pocket either.

If there's a boy handy, I have him hoist the end of the tape high above his head or fix him in my sight while he balances my seven-foot vernier. He stares back at me, his eyes to mine, and that stick can't help but adjust to vertical. For reward, I focus on, say, a birch protruding from a ridge of mountain miles away. Count the leaves, I dare him. He squints, peers through, glances at me, peers through again. He can't believe it, how close the branches of that white tree glisten. Sometimes a younger boy will extend his hand, nervous fingers reaching out as if to touch, but I don't laugh. I respect what he hasn't learned to hide.

My dad taught me the trade, and more often than not I use his words when I work because they still apply. He instructed my eye. One morning the year I became his journeyman, we were driving to a job in his Chevy. I was twenty, twenty-one at the time, still a kid, and thinking God knows what, when he called my attention to an abandoned field on the right.

What do you see, Frank, he asked me, and stopped the car.

There was nothing special. A pasture left fallow more than a few years—you could tell from the alder and maple saplings that had come back here and there—a loom of exposed ledge off to one side, a muddy rut where a culvert used to cut under the road.

Dad idled the truck to give me time. There was a depression in the weeds where once there had been a barnyard or a structure of some type. The grass all around had that yellow, wild color that appears when it hasn't been sowed fresh for too many seasons. Unbroken, the ground had turned tough, dense enough to seal a levee.

I'd sink a test at about thirty feet, I told Dad. Another halfways to the bank. We could conduct the overflow through a four-inch, and gravity would power it. With any luck we could go down six feet.

Five, he corrected, but he stepped on the gas, satisfied that my imagination would now fill any empty space with water.

He worked up to the week before he died, then left me his name and his equipment: A solid mahogany clipboard. A plane table. The glass with Swiss-ground lenses. It rests each night cushioned in its original case, in carved pockets lined with red velvet. The forged iron hammer. I've replaced the wooden handle, shattered once when anger got the better of me, but the head is as black and unmarred as if it never met a stake, never knew the flat of a nail.

I have his tape as well, that century-foot line of oiled cloth, mended with thread wherever ripped by sharp stones or roots. There've been some inches lost in the process, but it's still accurate enough. I used it until the printed numbers faded beyond recognition, then I wrapped it like a cast around my hand for the last time and stored it in the bottom drawer of my chest.

It bothers me, when I let it, that I've apprenticed no successor. My surviving children, Sam and Gloria, have moved with their families to other states. They work indoors, as was their ambition all along—he manages for Sears and she teaches school. They sleep in stone buildings with "interior windows" and "eternal fountains" in the lobbies. The seasons pass them by, blurred at the edges, of notice only on weekends. They never get so cold that they have to rub their toes, one at a time, or so warm that they fan the air with their hands. They never rise in the dark of the morning, never go to bed when it's still light. They heed clocks, my grown children, leave the world as they find it. They're content, but for their guilt over me since their mother passed away. I'm the loose board in their floor.

There's no right or wrong season for digging. You go in whenever the backhoe's free, and you're sure to fight something—hard crust in winter, swamp in spring, drought like as not the rest of the year. When I dam a pond site in late summer I forecast that the worst flood in a decade will sweep over the dusty rim. The runoff must have an escape, a waterfall if the contour of the bank will accommodate it. I sand the bottom, install a hydrant for fire protection. I insist on a minimum depth of eight feet. That way you can give up two for ice, allow another three for snow, and yet there'll remain sufficient oxygen in the water to keep trout alive.

Trout are the treasure of a healthy pond. They eat algae, you eat them. In summer, they can be lured to the surface to take food, and there's something fine about the way the light plays on those silver scales, crossing and reflecting like a handful of coins tossed in the air.

Sometimes, when we were courting and after we were new married, Martha would accompany me on an inspection. I bought her good boots, wool socks. Can't beat them. I explained each step of procedure and she nodded her head, interested, a quick study. She got so she could spot a bowl as well as I, foresaw the incline of slope, knew where to clear brush to make a view. It does her memory no disrespect to recall the use we put to certain warm afternoons, alone on what

5

would become the bed of the pond, the deepest pitch.

That first time, Martha surprised me. She blushed when I realized why she had brought the blanket from the foot of her bed, then she laughed at the look on my face. If you could see yourself, Frank, she said.

She was strong, tall as me, a year older. Her hair was straight and brown, the shade of river clay, and afterwards I would comb the straw from its tangle while she lay watching clouds, identifying their silhouettes. Sam was an April baby, full-size though two months premature as everyone consented to agree, but Martha and I knew for a fact he came from one of those excursions. Ben was two years later, a June after a late fall, so we suspected that origin of him as well.

We had thirty-eight years, Martha and I, and I was never with another woman, she was never with another man. That's the way it should be, I admonished Sam when he divorced Suzanne and married a second time. Not anymore, Dad, he answered me. You and Mom had no options. You played by the book and didn't question the rules.

Read your birth certificate and learn to count, I was tempted to say, but I held my tongue. The truth would sound like bragging. I let him believe what he needed, but his accusation brought Ben to my mind.

They say the second born gets lost by his parents,

that the middle child, being neither first nor last, becomes the independent one. Yet Ben was equal parts
Martha and me, in spirit as well as in form, as different
from Sam as fire from wood. He always had a question,
awoke with one in his mind, the leftover from his
dream, and he listened when you answered, he remembered what you said. He was good with his hands, fixed
things that were broken, located what was invisible to
everyone else. By the time he was seven he was my
number one. He had the eye, no question. He could
sense the vibration of water where it moved under lay-
ers of dry ground, could calculate on a sunny day the
route a rain spill might follow.

When my business settled into the black, I saved
enough to downpay twelve acres, then traded ponds for
the labor and materials it took to construct a house.
Our land had a southern exposure, a wooded knoll, but
not the trickle of a stream.

Where on the property do you want it situated? I
asked Martha before the frame was fully sided. There's
two choices, behind the house or beyond the hill for
privacy.

She stood in what would be her kitchen and faced
the space at hand through the bars of pine.

I don't see water in so close, she said. Too cramped a
pocket for my taste. Martha paused, caught my eye.
And I always valued privacy in a pond.

I smiled, recalled, approved her choice. The next day I burned two meadow acres and used the far side of our hill as the near embankment. When the depression filled, we could smell the water, hear it lap, only not behold it from our door.

The first summer was paradise. Gloria was two then, unsteady on her feet. She waded to her ankles and dropped pebbles to see the bubbles swell, while Martha and I watched the boys cannonball off a weighted plank. Some muggy nights, whispering on the stairs, Sam and Ben shut the door just so to keep from waking us, and stole outdoors to skinny-dip in the moonlight. Once I felt Martha's body stiffen as she prepared to call them back. They're good boys, I whispered, and stroked her arm the way she liked until instead she turned to me.

Ben, though younger, was the leader, and he was impatient with time. Clocks and calendars moved too slow for his ambition. Every day he was gone before breakfast, out of breath and home from school ten minutes when Sam walked through the front door. When the winter came, he couldn't wait for center ice to thicken to try his skates.

We shook our heads. He was late to dinner, the third time that week. We called the neighbor boy, his schoolmate, at seven, and he was missing also. By the time we thought where to search, the temperature had dropped, mending the hole, leaving as evidence only a glare in the shape of an explosion. I grabbed a pick, slammed it down and a pool broke through, then I dove into the darkness, calling his name until my mouth was filled. I touched the bottom with my palms—it was but ten feet—and encountered only silt, grainy as powder. But when I ascended, Ben blocked my entrance. Obedient and sorry, he had floated to the sound of our voices. Martha had already dragged his head and shoulders onto the cradle of her lap. His legs moved in the gentle waves, the steel of his skates clicking together in an undecipherable code.

I ran with him in my arms. Martha shouted a story of a boy who lived underwater in a frozen lake for close to an hour and was revived by immersion in a warm tub. She opened the tap while I lay Ben on the floor and pumped his lungs, pushing his back and raising his arms, bent like chicken wings. His body was cold to the touch, so logged it chafed as our skin rubbed together. The water overflowed and splashed the floor when Ben displaced it.

LATER, MEN CAME, DRAGGED THE pond, and found the neighbor boy. The two were buried side by side. No word of blame was hurled. None was needed. Everyone knew which man had dug the hole. Martha and I did the bare minimum for Sam and Gloria, and had nothing left. For weeks after the service, we hardly saw each other. I for one was fearful of what might erupt if we spoke.

You had to have the pond so far away, I might easily have unleashed, and then that accusation could never again be caged. *Privacy* was a word we struck from our vocabularies, and thereafter, when it was uttered by another, we averted our eyes from any connection.

I sat by the parlor stove, kept the coals red, the drapes drawn, and did not answer the knocks of those who came when I failed to walk their land. Martha spent her hours elsewhere. I was not curious, but at meals I saw she wore the same dress as on that night, its torn hem still unrepaired. One morning, I brought out my father's level, set the case before me on the table. I lifted the hammer, brought it down with such force that the handle split, but the metal box was made to last, and the Swiss glass did not shatter.

Ben was taken November twelfth. On December twelfth Martha opened the door, parted the curtains. She had changed her clothes and mashed her hair into a tight bun.

A month is all the mourning we shall indulge, she said. We have two remaining to us who will want their Christmas, and we're out of money. She grasped my hands, hauled me to my feet, and kept her hold as we faced each other, her breath beating on my cheek. She felt the tremble that started in my legs and worked its way up my body, but with a hard squeeze of her fingers, she dammed it, cinching it off the way you save a well by crimping a severed feeder pipe uncovered by a careless hoe.

We lived an ordinary life thereafter. Martha joined clubs of women and I worked steady. Even in hard times, and the county went through many, there were no lack of orders, no slack as people moved from cities and were willing to go into debt for their ideal. Those locals who knew my story never aired it, and if the new ones heard, they couldn't risk a question that might lose me. There was none other for a hundred miles trained to do my job, no other job I was trained to do. Necessity dictated amnesia and I stayed busy twenty years, every hour occupied, and I did quality work. First Sam and later Gloria showed no aptitude to follow me, the slant of their minds unpredictable and remote from my own. So I hired temporary assistants. I became less my father's son and more a man known for himself, in my own eyes as well as in the estimate of others.

I took for granted the patterns, the pathways worn by repetition. Divert a stream and eventually the shape of rocks will alter. Veins appear, then channels carved so deep they seem the natural order. I trusted in the warm wall of my wife beside me in sleep, in the last cup of evening coffee saved for breakfast and in the appearance of supper at five-thirty each night. My half of labor met and fit with Martha's. I depended on her sensible gifts—long johns and caps and heavy gloves—and gave her the same. We maintained our truce without ever declaring the war. And if something was missing, it was replaced by this reliability. We spared each other surprise, and each was grateful.

I expected I would go first. Men at sixty dropped all the time, survived by robust widows who improved their card playing, who became the backbone of the church. I had no fear. Death was not a polite topic. So when we went to the clinic for Martha's appointment I lacked premonition, was unprepared for the doctor's verdict. He had discovered a weakness in her circulation, an artery so tried that it might not long endure the pump of her heart. The condition was inoperable, he said. The weakness threaded into her brain beyond reach of the knife. The prognosis was unclear. It could burst at any time or last forever. She should avoid stress, take the pills he would prescribe, forget all worry if she could. She must not drive a car.

We walked to the parking lot in silence, embarrassed at this news. It was beyond our bounds. I turned the key, gripped the wheel.

Martha rested her hand on one of mine. Stop by the store on the way, she said. I have a list in my purse.

We didn't alert the children, adopted few changes in our routine. Any acknowledgment or compromise would make it real. We sold my Ford, because mine was older than hers. I tramped the ground each day, drew my geometric diagrams, satisfied my customers. On the surface, the nights with Martha were the same. We reported the news we had heard, we watched television after supper. We were careful of each other, but not so much we had to notice it.

We made a weir of habit that lasted almost a year, and gave the idea of death the time to settle, buried it from conscious thought the same as we had with Ben, or so I presumed. Martha saved her complaints for swollen ankles, for fingers that ached at the approach of rain. I lost my temper at chores. Railed when the sink was piled night after night with the caked pots Martha used for cooking, then left for me to scrub.

One evening, while she slept covered with an afghan on the couch, I had a craving and went to the freezer-box in the cellar for ice cream. I lifted the lid, propped it against the wall, and there before me were a month of meals, each neatly wrapped in dull foil and labeled with masking tape—stews, casseroles, succotash—and I understood the pots. I stared into that lighted chest, let the

13

cold wash my face, until above me I heard the tread of Martha's steps.

The lights flickered, I called. I'm down here to check the fuse. I never mentioned what I'd seen, but after that it got so we could talk in cautious ways, discuss arrangements, agree on plans. Martha took the lead and I listened, became the sounding board for her memory as she compiled albums of photographs for Sam and Gloria. She'd pass the snapshots to me, and I held them the length of my arm for sharper focus.

THE MESSAGE FROM THE HOSPITAL found me in a fenced quadrant, looking east through my sight. The day was overcast, warm. The soil was cracked and tan below the brown grass. It was a challenge, this property, for there were no natural outcrops in any direction. Either this pond would have to be much longer than was requested, or I'd have to force an artificial hollow into the land. I had paced for half an hour seeking some slight incline, some fixed basset where I could anchor a nail, but in the end I had no choice but to employ the door of Martha's car.

I parked at the terminus where the access road stopped, then measured eighty feet and set up my plane table. I sighted on the chrome knob of the handle, made it my hundred, stretched my chains. The perspective worked. I could see the completed pond in my mind, smaller than I had guessed, the water running before the breeze. Now the trick would be to locate again the exact same benchmark, to distinguish that precise point of origin from all the other impossible places, when I came back to dig.

EARNEST
MONEY

WHEN I CROSSED THE BORDER on foot at Scobey six months after the general amnesty, and two weeks after Dad passed on, no brass bands were playing—but then, it was a well-known fact that even the actual vets didn't get parades. It was a typical eastern Montana March day—wind that took a running start at the mountains, then raced across the plains to cut your skin like stiff paper. There's a way the land rolls along the Hi-line—one rise blinding into the next —that makes it look like sky turned hard. Outcrops of rock are gray as bone and you're just in the middle of it all, one more thing blowing from nowhere to anywhere. It's the kind of place you either love because you haven't gone away, or love for the simple reason that you have—and are relieved to be back.

I stood in the U.S. Customs booth, getting my bearings. I declared myself an American citizen, listed my mom's house in Galata as my permanent address, said I had been in Canada on vacation, and swore I had nothing of material value to declare. The dude rubbed his pencil against his cheek, looked me up and down. What did he see? I was just another long drink of water, my hair pulled back in a ponytail, my Grateful Dead T-shirt tucked into faded Wranglers, a pair of Keds that had seen cleaner days. If he didn't inquire how long I'd been away—nine years was a lot of vacation to explain—I was free and clear.

"Where'd you graduate from?" he asked.

"Milk River."

The man raised his eyebrows. I'd seen such tests on TV. Next he'd want to know who won the World Series in 1952 or what was the capital of Missouri. But the fact was, the man was merely starved for conversation.

"Class of . . . ?"

" 'Sixty-seven." Here came the big one: Where'd I serve?

"Then you must have known Earl Stromeier, year behind you? I played hoops against his brother Marky."

"Do tell."

"What do you hear of Earl?"

I shook my head. I didn't hear of anybody.

"Somebody mentioned he went down to Billings. Lives in a condo with a swimming pool."

I cocked my head to show polite amazement. The two facts that came back to me about Earl were that he wore a flag on the flap of his jean jacket and that he was a regular viewer of "Gilligan's Island." He used to imitate the rich old guy, the one who was Mr. Magoo's voice, but he wasn't very good at it.

"Earl always had ambition," I agreed, and that was enough to pass me through.

So, how did I feel being returned at last? This was a moment I had pictured more than once. I had imagined I'd stop feeling like a stranger, stop having to explain my whys and wherefores to anyone who wanted to know, stop being surprised at where I found myself. I stood still and paid attention. South of the border the pavement changed from black to gray, plus the distances got shorter because they were reported in miles instead of kilometers. According to the road sign, I hadn't traveled as far as I thought.

Exhaust was spewing from the tail pipe of the one idling automobile, a green Pontiac with two women in the front seat and another in the back. The driver was Mom, but she didn't fling open her door at the sight of her only child. Instead, she pointed in my direction. The friend in the backseat wagged her head and patted Mom's shoulder. I walked over to the rolled-up window and knocked.

Mom pressed a button and the glass lowered partway, as though she was going to ask directions of a stranger of whom she was more than a little uncertain. Her eyes were invisible behind her shades, so I made the first move.

"Guess who?"

"Don't you have luggage?"

"I mailed a box. You know me: travel light."

Mom sighed, as if this news confirmed her worst fears. The rear door opened and one of Mom's bridge club regulars got out.

"Mrs. Marion." I nodded, recognizing her from my past life.

She smiled, pleased that I had remembered her name, then caught herself and made a pinched face. "You'll have to ride in the middle, Sky," she announced, employing the name people have called me since sixth grade, Sky. "Even with your long legs. I get carsick over the hump, and the cooler will only fit if it's against the door, so it has to be you."

"You bet." I scooted in. The air was a combination

of heater, cigarettes, and toilet water, battled to a tie score. I settled down and treated myself to a behind-the-scenes inspection of Mom's head. Her hair was collected into a netted bun, and the dark right lens of her glasses confronted me from the mirror. It occurred to me, not for the first time, that she had never once visited while I lived in Canada.

"New wheels?" I smoothed the plush upholstery and rested my feet on the matching rubber mat that flowed over the drive shaft.

"Death benefits," Mrs. Marion accused in a whisper, reminding me that I was now half an orphan.

That was the last word exchanged for the next seventy miles. On the car radio, "The Farm Report" was followed by "The Holy Redeemer Half-Hour," and that by "Swap, Shop, or Barter." There were lots of call-ins who wanted to unload handyman's specials or like-new stereo AM/FM eight-track tape decks with quadraphonic sound, and one set of dishes with only two salads missing, but no takers.

After the first twenty miles, Mrs. Marion got the urge for a smoke. She tapped a Salem from a snap case in her purse and held it over the emergency brake until Mom pushed the lighter into the dashboard. When it popped out, Mrs. Marion leaned across the seat, clamped the filtered end of the cigarette in her mouth, pressed the other against the red coil, and inhaled three or four deep huffs. Then she sat back and blew a long burst of thanks. There was an ashtray, half full, built into the side of her door.

Shy of Wolf Point I tried to change the subject of the disgrace of my being a draft dodger. "Earl Stromeier's moved to Billings," I said.

"Earl's schooling was paid for by V.A. benefits," volunteered Mrs. Marion, and dug for another smoke. I got the point. You wouldn't find Earl riding in the middle.

I couldn't place Mom's front-seat companion, but I was interested in the way she held her head arched back, like the hammer on a pistol, ready to fire. She had the look of a shop teacher I once knew who had no patience for excuses—of which, he had often reminded me, I was a poor example.

"Personally, it wouldn't hurt my feelings a bit to see Canada." The mystery woman had a raspy voice, and though her announcement was technically addressed to me as a recent resident of Saskatchewan, it was Mom's face she watched. Her cheeks tightened in satisfaction when Mom shot her a stabbed-in-the-heart glance.

"Evelyn," Mrs. Marion hushed. "Think." Evelyn looked back at me and pulled down one corner of her mouth to show she had previously done just that. I noticed she was more my age than Mom's.

"It's a beautiful country," I said. "I'd be glad to

show it to you sometime, though I take no responsibility for the weather."

"I've got a suitcase packed," Evelyn muttered under her breath.

That day I thought she was merely using a figure of speech, but it happened she was serious. Later, at home, when I asked for the lowdown, Mom mouthed the word "divorced."

"Anybody I knew?"

"Dale Unger? From over to Culbertson? Solid as a brick, but I guess that's not enough for some." Mom was a defender of the matrimonial state. She had often confided that she had endured more than most would bear in order to uphold her vows.

My interest in Evelyn increased, now that I knew she was a fugitive from civilized society.

"Well, was she just along for the ride today or what?"

Mom shrugged, her shoulders slow and heavy with meaning, and brought the conversation back to where she wanted it. "It's my curse," she said. "I feel sorry, try to be nice. And look what it gets me."

Dad, she really meant, and now me. I nodded in sympathy.

"She's Betty Marion's cousin," Mom continued. "Come visiting to lick her wounds."

Songs play in my head all the time, one after the

other, as if my brain is a dish pointed at an invisible satellite. Mostly I find the volume's set a peg too low for me to make out all the words. This time, however, I caught a few definite bars of a new tune, and it sounded not one bit bad at all.

MOM EXPECTED THAT I'D TAKE up where I left off. Actually, somewhat beyond that point. Without Dad around, Mom was horsepower with nothing to move. She took my stay in a foreign country as indication of an aptitude for political science. She had big plans for my enrollment at Northern State College and was triple-pissed when I declined to fill out the application forms she had sent for.

In fact, she was still barely speaking to me on Monday morning when we went downtown to collect my inheritance. Either Dad had forgiven me my desertion or he had put off too long making good his parting threat to cut me out of his will, because there was an account with thirteen thousand dollars of insurance money drawing interest in my name. I figured I might as well put it to work, though on what I couldn't say. Still, if it was in my pocket, it'd be handy when an idea blossomed.

Mom, of course, despaired of this plan and reminded me of all the months Dad paid into the premium, all the things she went without, never complaining, like reusing a paper towel at least once before throwing it away and limiting herself to a solitary teaspoon of instant coffee on weekdays.

So first thing out of the bank I steered her into the Do-Re-Me and ordered us each a bottomless cup while we considered the menu.

"You think you're funny," Mom whispered. "Well, you're not."

Funny wasn't what I was after. Somewhere along the line I had decided it was easier to concede a point than to argue it, to give freely what people said they wanted and to wish for their happiness. This was a theory I held on to against the evidence of my experience. Mom was a case in point. She had claimed on the telephone that her dearest hope was that I would come back and be company for her, but now that I had, she didn't know what to do with me.

I ordered pie to celebrate, me the huckleberry and Mom the sour cream raisin. Then, while we were waiting for it to appear, I glanced out the window and there was Evelyn looking in. She didn't give me the chance to wave, just walked through the door and occupied the empty chair next to me as if the meeting had been set up in advance. Mom's back went straighter, and I signaled for another place setting.

"What'll it be?" I asked Evelyn.

She lifted her chin, surveyed the options posted along the wall, and chose the liver plate.

"I eat what I don't make," she told us. "I'd rather spend my time at a good double feature than slice onions."

Mom was in a condition of mental arrest, the two causes for it tied for number one.

"It's eleven o'clock in the morning," she protested. Then, taking a short breath, she added, "That meat could have been sitting here for a week."

Evelyn's answer was to make her eyes big, as though she was a concerned third-party observer—a technique that threw off Mom's timing. I made a note to remember to use it, and reached for the brown envelope the bank had given me.

"What do you think?" I asked Evelyn, and dumped out the thirteen thousand dollars, all neat in stacks with paper bands around them, on her Summer Pleasures of Montana place mat. Mom flapped a napkin over my fortune, but not before Evelyn had nodded.

"Spending money is a thing I want to learn how to do," she said, and patted her purse. "I've got a stash of my own, and it's the only damn thing I have to show for eighteen years of living death."

You wouldn't call Evelyn small. Her shoulders were

rounded beneath a lavender windbreaker, and her legs, short and thick, disappeared into scuffed brown boots. Her hair, coarse and graying at the temples, was cropped shorter than mine, and from each of her earlobes there dangled a gold hoop that, on closer inspection, turned out to be a coiled snake eating its own tail. She wore no makeup and smelled like soap. Her hazel eyes were her most startling feature. It was their brightness, as if she had a two-hundred-watt light bulb lit behind them. She could have stood in the middle of a dark church and brightened up the farthest corner.

Nobody approved when Evelyn and I started going out. Mom and her friends warned me that she was on the rebound, that who I was didn't matter, that I could have been anybody in pants— which is pretty much what I was. They said I should meet more people, that they could fix me up with a fine girl more my age who worked at a job with a health plan. I didn't say yes and I didn't say no, but all the while they were bragging about Blue Cross and dental work, I was wondering how Evelyn would look with her face relaxed.

For some time, she herself refused to acknowledge my interest, pretending it was pure coincidence when I took the seat next to hers at the local movie house the night of our lunch. And why shouldn't we share a bite afterwards? For certain, we each packed enough cash to pay half a check.

For a while we arranged to run into each other accidentally. At the end of an evening, I'd wait for her to drop mention of a future destination, and then the next night there we'd both be at the Steerio Lounge or Bowl-Till-You-Drop. It took a good month for me to call her at her cousin's, and when I did, I learned something new: Evelyn might pick up a telephone if it rang, but she declined to be the first to speak.

"Hello," I said to dead air.

"What?"

"You want to shack up?" I asked, surprising myself. I had intended to ask Evelyn if she wanted to drive over to Shelby and eat spaghetti, but suddenly that seemed too small a question for her irritated tone of voice.

More dead air.

"Well?" I asked again. There was no use making like she had heard me wrong.

"You'll be sorry," was all she answered.

Those were exactly the words that Mom employed when I broke the news, followed on the heels by, "Thank God your father didn't live to see this day."

"Would you rather we got married first?"

Mom filled her whistling teapot with water and slammed it on the stove to boil. "Are those my two choices? Marriage or sin?"

I said I guessed so.

"What does *she* want to do?"

The next day I asked, and soon found out.

"Once was one time too many," Evelyn stated, and put the subject of matrimony to bed.

E VELYN REGULARLY GOT PUT OUT by the dreams that came to her just before she woke. On the dawn of the second morning in our furnished apartment over the movie house, she complained that she had been walking through a yard sale, her arms loaded with bargains, when the property owners changed their minds, told the browsers to put everything back where they found it and go home. Evelyn's eyes had snapped open and her arms were folded tight across her chest. It took three cups of black coffee and my complete silence to shift her back into neutral.

Certain days, she had long periods of seething, when her peace of mind came as rare as a crowbar of sun from an overcast sky. When those moods arrived at bedtime, she'd start on the edge of the mattress, tuck one end of the blanket under her arm, then roll herself into a tight cigar of exasperation. It was too hot. It was too cold. It was noisy. It was stuffy. Her life's disappointments were a grocery list of wrongs that she refused to talk about.

"Just nod if I'm right," I said one night about two A.M. "It's got something to do with your divorce settlement."

Her head didn't budge an inch, but her eyes narrowed.

I tried putting the words into her mouth. "You got cheated out of what was coming to you."

If Evelyn had been still before, now she was a stone fence.

"It's something *I* did." My last blind guess.

She blinked, unclenched her features for a fraction of a second. "Don't flatter yourself."

It's hard to explain, but I took it as a compliment first that she answered me, and second that I wasn't at the seat of her problem. Having that fact confirmed, knowing I was out of the direct line of her fire, made it bearable when, her lips pressed into a grim seam, she'd turn away from my kisses. What it meant was, I wasn't just anybody in pants. I was more like the exception to Evelyn's general rule: a person worth explaining to, a person whose feelings Evelyn as soon wouldn't hurt, all things being equal. Special.

Sometimes I caught her watching me with more pleasure than pain—and that beats all the poetical words in the dictionary. You might say Evelyn's suspicion of happiness was a challenge I rose to in a contest she didn't entirely declare to be out of my league. It was a long shot: nobody, not even her, would blame me if I failed—though sometimes, I'll allow, she seemed to be betting against me. She kept her suitcase in plain view. She expected me to find fault with the strange frozen food she served, with the housekeeping she despised, with the positions she warned me were off-limits in bed. No matter what I did or didn't do, Evelyn hung to the reins of her doubts as tight as she did to the money she wouldn't spend. She kept herself ready to be the first one of us to say that she didn't give a shit.

The thing was, I recognized her bossiness for what it was: the instruction booklet that up to then my life had been lacking. It was a relief for questions to come with the decisions already made, to have firm opinions to rub against. After passing so many fair days, Evelyn was a thunderstorm that knocked out all competing electricity.

B EARPAW LAKE STATE PARK WAS twenty miles west of town, and one hot May afternoon Evelyn and I drove over in her car to sightsee. I was glad for the chance, since I hadn't been in water deeper than a bathtub since 1968. Of course, Evelyn wouldn't go near the beach—she said it reminded her of her honeymoon trip to Hawaii—so while I cooled off she walked over to check out the administration buildings. We rendezvoused on the picnic grounds two hours later.

"You missed a good time," I told her. "I'm a new man."

"And I'm on the payroll," she stated. "Meet the staff cook."

"You hate to cook," was my first reaction.

"I hate to cook for *me*," Evelyn corrected. "I hate to do anything for free. Getting paid is another story. Besides, what else do I know how to do? Can you see me in a store? Selling dresses?"

I tried to imagine Evelyn behind a counter with an inviting smile on her face, but the image scrambled, like a TV picture during a blizzard.

"When do you start?" I asked.

"An hour ago. This is my break. We can't go home until I feed them supper."

When Evelyn went back to the kitchen I sat under a tree, watching the light play on the little waves. There was a part of me that minded how she went about her business as though it had nothing to do with me. We had plenty of money to live on and the subject of employment had never come up. I had held down jobs of every description in Regina, from construction to checkout register to maintenance, but they all had in common the same drawback. The truth was, what I hated about working wasn't the working, it was the working *for.*

But on the other hand I couldn't very well sit home and count dustballs while Evelyn fed a crew. Her decision to get hired presented me with a far-reaching dilemma: to follow her or be left behind. I was at a crossroads similar to the one I had faced before, but that time it was go or go or go, Vietnam or Canada or the pen. All I was left with was wondering which one would be worse, and that turned out to be not so hard. Now, as I tried to figure out what to do with my life next, all I kept getting through the static of my possibilities was the echo of that word *home* from Evelyn's mouth. That was answer enough.

I had hours to kill, so after a while I got up, followed the gravel path down to the park entrance. The cars raced east and west, exceeding the speed limit. Finally one of them, a blue Chevy with Oregon plates, slowed down as it approached where I stood. I thought at first they were going to offer me a lift—I'd never been to Oregon—but their goal was staring me in the face: across the highway was a red and white Conoco station. The driver of the Chevy and I noticed at the same instant that the place was deserted, with a FOR SALE sign posted in the window. This news caused him to speed back up, to look further, but it had the reverse effect on me. At the first break in traffic, I crossed the road.

Interested parties were directed to dial a number and inquire at Deja-View Realtors. I used the pay phone attached to the side of the building, and was encouraged to find that it still worked.

"Deja-View. Irma." The voice was cheerful but firm, ready for anything.

"The Conoco at Bearpaw? What do they want for it?"

"Twenty thousand?" Irma answered as though she was asking me.

"Cash?"

"This is George, isn't it?" she demanded. I recognized her tone from TV shows—it was how people sounded on "Candid Camera" when they began to suspect the truth of their circumstance.

"I've got thirteen thousand in my back pocket this minute," I said to reassure her.

"Sandy?"

"My name is Sky Dial," I said. "I'm here at the station as we speak."

There was a pause on the other end of the line while

Irma waited for me to add more, to give myself away. When I didn't, her voice changed back to where it had started.

"Don't budge a step, honey. I'm on my way."

It took Irma fifteen minutes, but that gave me time to inspect the property on my own—except I didn't know what I should be looking for. The plate glass of the office part was streaked and dirty, and the lock was broken on the men's room. The sink inside had a brown stain under the dripping faucet of the cold, which spelled iron in the water. I assumed that Irma would not expect me to have uncovered this drawback, and so I felt at an advantage when I heard her car pull in. DEJA-VIEW was stenciled in white on the green metallic paint.

"Sky?" Irma held out her hand to be shook. She was a compact woman dressed Western, that is, pointy boots, a shirt with snaps instead of buttons, and a fringed suede vest. Her hair was blond and beauty parlor–arranged with unlikely rises and falls. Compared to her I felt seedy, untucked in, so I touched my pocket and mentioned the iron problem.

"Nothing some Comet won't cure," Irma said. "But I'm glad you noticed. That means you'll be a proprietor who keeps the place up. This location is a gold mine. It commands the park. Nobody can get in or out without passing your pumps."

Or by, I thought. People from as far away as Oregon were disappointed not to stop, but I didn't want to betray this insight. The way Irma described the Conoco put me in mind of a fort, and that recalled the customs booth on the border where this all began, and that made me think of Mom in her car and how she would feel about me spending Dad's insurance money this way instead of on an A.A. degree.

"You quoted twenty thousand?"

"That's the *asking* price." Irma leaned toward me to share a secret. "I happen to know that the owner is desperate. Make a reasonable offer."

"What would you call 'reasonable'?"

Irma lowered her voice still further. "Knock off ten percent." Her eyes darted to the right and left. She didn't want to be overheard selling short her client just because she wanted to help me out. "Fifteen."

I figured the arithmetic in my head. Even at this bargain-basement rate I was still short four bills, and I confessed as much.

"You could put down earnest money to freeze the property," Irma, my new best friend, advised.

"What's that?" The term was news to me.

"A simple deposit. No risk to you since it's all returned if you're unable to secure financing. But this way you won't run the gamble of another buyer moving in while you assemble your assets. You'll hold the exclusive right to purchase for ten business days." She paused, bent closer. "I happen to know that a couple from California has an appointment to view this station with another agent later this very week."

We both knew what California meant. I could see the couple, tan and rich. They wouldn't hesitate to act, but I could still ace them out.

"I'm obliged by law to tell you, though," Irma stated, "that there may be a penalty for changing your mind. If you harbor any doubt, only put down what you can afford to lose."

I thought of Mom throwing up her hands in despair. I thought of Evelyn, not a ten-minute walk distant, probably peeling potatoes at this very moment. I thought of me, wearing a uniform at last, guarding the entrance to Bearpaw Lake. I knew the words were right when I heard myself say them.

"Draw up the papers. Will you take twelve thousand down?"

"But that's too . . ." Irma began, then shook her hair, laughed at her own caution. "Sky, you're a man who knows his mind."

E VELYN HAD NEVER TOLD ME HOW much she had to show from her marriage and I had never asked. I was afraid to now, but I had no choice since I couldn't go to Mom, and the banker was convinced I was mental after I had closed out my whole account.

"A pump jockey?" Evelyn and I were stopped at the station so that she could see for herself the advantages of the location. She clamped her mouth as if to hold my proposal steady and get a better view. Then she let it float free. "Well, I guess you've got to do something."

She looked tired after her afternoon of labor, like some of the fire had gone out of her.

"I'm short five thousand. It'd be in both our names."

Evelyn turned toward me in the seat, her face flushed, her eyes glittery in sudden anger.

"Take it from me. Joint property doesn't count for shit."

"This time it will," I promised. "Live and learn."

Evelyn considered what I said but didn't change her expression. She spoke in a voice that scratched the air.

"I have a daughter. Had one."

"Did something happen to her? Did she die?"

Evelyn shifted her body, stared into the windshield. Her hands were clasped together in her lap.

"Dead to me," she said. "She stayed."

I started the engine and nosed the car onto the highway. We drove back to town in silence, and as the miles rolled by I didn't know if through this revelation we were broke up or broke through.

"It wouldn't be that way with us," I finally offered in my own defense.

"You're not doing this for yourself," she thought out loud. "It's all because you don't want to be left alone."

I didn't deny this fact, so it came down to whether for Evelyn this was welcome news or bad, her call. She could leave me or take me along for the ride.

INSTEAD OF SIGNING A CONTRACT between us, making it a loan, Evelyn and I got married after all. The only things she hated worse than judges were lawyers and priests, so we stood in Mom's living room before the lesser of the three evils.

I wouldn't call the reception a wild celebration, not by any means. From the point of view of the guests it was a mix of "too bad" and "it could be worse" with a little bit of "what the hell" thrown in on the side. Mom had insisted on hosting, saying it was more civilized than us greeting the world in the used mobile home that was Evelyn's and my wedding gift to ourselves. Besides, the familiarity of her friends gave Mom strength, and Mrs. Marion could provide the live entertainment—a rendition of double-hand keyboard favorites.

Evelyn wore a dark red dress and matching shoes, and her hair was clinched in a tight permanent that would take weeks to loosen up. With her thumb she kept turning the gold band on her finger, a ring bought with the last of Dad's insurance. She sat with her feet apart and pressed onto the floor, her shoulders hunched. She appeared to take so little pleasure, and I dearly wanted her to feel like me: lucky.

Evelyn's normal eyes were so pale compared to the rest of her when she wasn't angry that you didn't notice them at first. But today they were little girl's eyes, alarmed to find themselves in a grown woman's face. Their expression reminded me of someone who had just woken up and couldn't place where she was. Without moving her head, her glance raced around the room, then stopped at the window, drank up the sun. At my touch on her arm, Evelyn turned toward me, her whole body tensed, ready to defend itself. Her lips parted, she drew a breath. But her eyes, her eyes weren't at all sure what to think.

QIANA

SOME NIGHTS THE SNOW THAT
fell in Dunlop, New Hampshire, was a dusting, a cover
draped like a thin sheet over old furniture. Other nights
it packed wet and tight, creating new contours that
melded the overhang of garage roofs with the top posts
of fences and made the sweep of fields smooth as the
lakes of the moon.

Mornings after such storms, Normand Pasco
hunched on the seat of the town plow and dealt with
the night's damage. Years ago he had devised a schedule

for his stretch of Route 11, and he held to it. At fifty-five, he had the chapped face and bent-inward body of a man who had passed much of his life in bad weather. His wife Irene was shorter, boxy and solid, yet hard to pin down as rain in midair. She managed Normand the way she managed appointments for a group of doctors in another town—with an efficiency rooted in disdain.

There were no children to the match—even a dog could have thrown off the balance that Normand and Irene had evolved over eighteen years. Theirs was the kind of arrangement a twin brother and sister might concoct, the kind where two people had read each other's minds so long they had lost interest in the novelty. Normand was Irene's extra pair of hands when she needed something to be moved, and she was his reference library, the book he consulted to remember whether he liked his T-bone medium or medium-well.

Monday through Friday, work schedules kept Normand and Irene apart, and even on weekends they rarely met without purpose: he cruised the roads scouting for potholes or soft shoulders, and she restocked the pantry and did the wash.

IN THE TEN YEARS SINCE MARILYN Dixon's ex-husband had departed, her grown son Arthur had become more companion than child, replacing his father as the primary audience of her comments, the chief object of her improvements, the subject of the sighing complaints she confided to other women . . . until, in the early fall of 1991, Arthur was laid off from his job at Split Ball-Bearing. Unemployment checks temporarily anchored him to Dunlop, but when they stopped arriving he quit threatening to leave his mother's house and relocate to Arizona, and did.

For sixty days, Marilyn refused to digest that she lacked a male to do for. She rose at six-fifteen every morning as if she still had to wake Arthur for work, and discussed him with her bridge partners as though he had just stepped out for an evening at the Cinema One-Two-Three. Then a postcard of a Holiday Inn arrived from Scottsdale that read: *I'm not registered here but this was free. I've got a job at an electronic car wash in Phoenix and met somebody. Think of me when it snows. Ha ha.*

When Marilyn ran into Irene coming out of the post office, she automatically showed her the card. Irene studied the message longer than it took to read it, and when she finally raised her eyes, Marilyn detected boredom, the edge of pity. As if a light had just switched on in a dark basement, Marilyn's affectionate attitude toward her son abruptly reversed, and soon thereafter, a hand-lettered page announcing a Saturday rummage sale appeared on the bulletin board at Cartiers' Quick Stop.

W HEN IRENE AND NORMAND ARRIVED at Marilyn's house shortly after two o'clock, the lawn was already crowded. They joined in the procession, moving from item to item, turning upside down, pricing almost before noticing what they held, the left-behinds of Marilyn's husband and son. If she bought, Irene's down-turned mouth and frowning brows communicated, it would not be from desire. Normand followed in her wake, tolerant and uncomfortable. He nodded to other husbands, removed his cap often and then replaced it. Shopping was a wife's province. He was here only to carry her purchases.

Marilyn's yard was raked into a perfect grid, and she'd arranged the goods for sale carefully as if they were treasures in a room preserved behind velvet ropes. To wander among them was to take a trip in a time machine: campaign buttons from every presidential candidate who had entered the New Hampshire primary, from Kennedy and Nixon to Ronald Reagan; a picked-over stack of Red Sox baseball cards; out-of-order *National Geographic*s. In one box, optimistically titled "Scissors Fun for the Kids," were piled all the glossy Christmas, birthday, and Valentine's cards Arthur had given to his mother over the years.

Menswear labeled in various sizes was strung on a plastic line—U.S. Army fatigues, a black suit, a battered goosedown parka, long underwear "Ideal for Rags." For the lack of anything better to do, Normand riffled through the clothes, arriving finally at a cluster bound on one side by a beige Nehru jacket and on the other by three pairs of bell-bottom pants. One garment in particular was so bright it was impossible to miss. In fact, so many surprised browsers had pushed aside faded chamois and plaid cottons to get a better view that it had become isolated, showcased.

It was a shirt from a moment so precisely in the center of the 1970s that it might have been assigned a calendar date, a shirt whose top two buttons were never intended to close, a shirt whose silky synthetic fabric was meant to slip against a suntanned chest offset with a gold chain, a shirt that, by the time it had been purchased new at Johnny's Clothiers in Laconia, had gone out of style everywhere else in the world.

Normand's eyes followed the recurring jagged design as it raced in horizontal peaks and valleys, each outlined in a contrasting bright color. The effect was first blue, then pink, then a kind of purple—hypnotic in the way of a spinning mirror or a flashing jewel. The shirt spoke to him, though he couldn't have spelled out the message, and he peered at it the way a farsighted man squints at something close up and very fine. Safety-pinned to the tail was a small square of yellow paper that read, "Rarely Used/$4."

Irene had inspected half the soles in a box of un-matched shoes before she realized she was alone.

"Normand?" She didn't interrupt the thrust of her dig for a size-ten right snow boot. When she got no reply, her head jerked up and she saw that her husband was blocking traffic. Curious that she had failed to command his attention by the force of her will, she recrossed the yard, left boot in hand.

"See something you like?" Marilyn was there ahead of Irene, prepared to do business.

Normand nodded toward the shirt so suddenly and sharply that he felt dizzy. Both women followed his gesture, and Marilyn lifted the hanger off the line.

"It's genuine Qiana." Her voice was soft, almost reverent, but there was a thirty-volt current in it. "It'll become you. Arthur only wore it a couple times."

"Must have been in hot summer," Irene observed, pointing her chin at a perspiration stain under one arm.

"Qiana is delicate." Marilyn's tone suggested that Irene was a stranger to delicates. "I used color-safe powder bleach but it still ran."

"It wasn't the only one." Irene leaned to read the price tag and then straightened from the waist up. "You must be dreaming."

But Normand already had his gloves off and his wallet buckled in the palm of one hand. He licked two fingers, counted out four bills one at a time, and handed them to Marilyn.

"At least try it on first," his wife ordered.

Normand took the shirt from the hanger and folded it into a neat square. Irene drew a deep breath and bought a desk lamp she didn't need for more money than she planned to spend. Five minutes later at the snack table she mistakenly stirred sugar instead of powdered creamer into her coffee. Finally, empty-handed except for the lamp, she walked back to her car, Normand by her side as if nothing out of the ordinary had happened.

NORMAND HAD NEVER PREVIOUSLY felt the need to provide himself with a retreat. At home, he tended to divide his time between the kitchen and the living room, depending on the offering of food or television. Yet that afternoon, in the chill of Irene's disapproval, he was awkward as an extra piece of furniture, so eventually he sought privacy behind the one door that could be locked. He let the tap in the bathroom sink run full force, stripped off his sweater and white cotton undershirt, and tried on Arthur's shirt. The weightless material was sleek and cool beneath his fingers as he undid each button. It clung to the bare skin of his shoulders with the magnetism of static electricity and coated each of his forearms almost as if the fabric were wet. Normand tucked the tail into his pants, sucked in his stomach, and hitched his belt, then turned to see the effect.

The image that confronted him was framed by a continuous row of frosted globes. In their glare, Normand looked embalmed. His lips were too red, his eyes too small and deep-set. His ears did not lie close enough against his head unless he pressed them back. On his brow, Normand noticed for the first time that there ran seams deep as scars. He tilted his chin and turned his head, left to right.

"You're wasting water," Irene called from the hall.

Normand changed out of the shirt, washed his hands, and rubbed his cheeks with a towel until he raised some color.

"It fit," he said, and slid the bolt.

To HIS NEIGHBORS, NORMAND WAS more familiar than popular. He asked no questions when he dropped in at Cartiers' for coffee the following Monday morning, engaged in no small talk. An overnight sleet had slicked the pavement, and the only questions addressed to Normand had to do with the distribution of salt on the highway. But something caught the eye of two regulars at the counter: a polished sheen at Normand's throat and a glimmer at the wrists of his parka.

"Hey, hey," Dale Cross said to Bill Taylor. "It's Willie Nelson."

"It's too *old* for Willie Nelson," joked back Bill. "It's Willie Nelson's ugly uncle."

"What's got a hundred and twenty pairs of legs and arms and no teeth?" Dale challenged.

"Front row of a Nelson concert," Dale replied.

Bill and Dale hooted once and glanced at each other, waiting for Normand to join in, but when he didn't they went back to their coffee.

To Normand, however, the room suddenly seemed too small, the ceiling too low, the light too dim, and all through the rest of that raw morning, as out of habit he drove the crosshatch of county roads and secondaries, his mood deepened. Finally, with no place else to go, he parked on the slight incline in front of Marilyn Dixon's house.

She opened her front door so immediately that it was clear she had been watching from a window. Backlit in the entranceway, her bouffant hair formed a reddish aura around her head.

She smiled.

Normand had in his mind an innocent favor to offer: he'd plow Marilyn's driveway. It was a task he performed occasionally for neighbors when time permitted, nothing personal about it, but before he got the words out, Marilyn saw through the gap in his unbuttoned jacket, marched into the cold, and found the shirt with the tips of her nails. At first her touch was merely the measure of recognition, but then she grasped a small pinch of material between her thumb and forefinger, made a friction of the satiny surface, and tugged.

IRENE HAD NEVER ANTICIPATED THAT she'd be the object of public sympathy, and found the role a nuisance. Women to whom she had barely spoken in the past began to drop by unannounced. She'd catch expressions on their faces that reminded her of when one of the M.D.'s where she worked assured a terminal patient that everything would be all right.

Irene pulled the drapes and took the phone off the hook those two or three nights a week when Normand was late coming home, and then arrived cleaner than when he'd left in the morning. Alone in the house, she turned the TV to The Weather Channel and marked the progress of storms as they worked their way east, through the mountains, through the plains, toward New Hampshire, and then beyond.

Mʏ ʙᴜꜱɪɴᴇꜱꜱ ɪꜱ ᴍʏ ʙᴜꜱɪɴᴇꜱꜱ," Normand told Marilyn as he sat at her kitchen table on the afternoon of New Year's Eve, delaying as long as possible the duty to go home.

"Why disappoint them?"

"Don't start."

"I *will* start. Why should we miss our first New Year's Eve just because of people with small minds?"

"What's so special about a plate of ham and baked beans?"

"New Year's out with you is like a tollbooth I want to pass through into the future."

Normand shook his head and smiled, in spite of himself. Marilyn sometimes said things so odd they were beyond argument. She could wake him up like the jolt of a frost heave on an otherwise smooth grade.

"It's not as though anyone will be shocked," Marilyn continued. She poured Normand a cup of coffee and automatically added half-and-half and two spoons of sugar the way she preferred it, even though he ordinarily took his black. "It'll be a relief for the pretense to be behind us."

Normand stood up, pushed the chair into its place against the table, pulled the gloves from his pocket and put them on, making a fist with each hand, then flexing his fingers. "Irene said if I showed up with you she'd change the locks."

"Well, you've got my key here. Hold on a minute with those gloves." She reached into the pocket of her velvet robe and held out a small box wrapped in foil. "Belated Merry Christmas, sweetheart."

The package was light in Normand's palm. It had been a long time since he had opened something without knowing in advance what was inside. Carefully, so as not to tear the paper, he slit each strip of clear tape with a fingernail, prolonging the moment. He enjoyed the feel of Marilyn's gaze, sensed her reaction to even the slightest movement of his hands as he uncovered a velvet jeweler's case that snapped open with the press of a button. Stuck within, embedded in white silk, was a ring.

"It's five carat," Marilyn explained. "And that's a star sapphire, the color of your eyes. Raise it to the light and look into the center. Can you tell the star?"

Normand studied the stone, turned it side to side,

then held it steady. Beneath the smooth, murky dome there seemed to float a suggestion: pale light from all directions joined in a midpoint, as if at a great, mysterious depth.

D RESSED IN A NEW RED AND WHITE houndstooth pantsuit, Irene arrived at the town hall alone at six-fifteen. Her face had pulled itself into straight lines and her hair was wound into a tight French twist. She had taken pains with her offering, and carried two pans of butterscotch supreme brownies, each individual square decorated with walnuts in the shape of a smiling face. Once at her assigned station behind the dessert table, she met the eyes of all who dared to look up. There was an intensity about her, a hum, and no one who worked their way down the buffet declined the scrape of her spatula.

The pattern of Normand's footsteps, though complicated by the counterpoint of his companion's high heels, was distinct and recognizable to Irene the moment he entered the door to her right. She did nothing, but those browsing among the cakes, pies, and ambrosia went on full alert. The rise of dough in a bowl would have been audible.

Irene shrugged a well-intentioned hand from its grasp of her elbow. She fixed her gaze on the floor before the table, followed the progress of two pairs of shoes as they shuffled sideways, almost in step, down the length of the white paper cloth. Eventually they stopped directly in front of her.

"Irene."

For a week, Irene had persuaded herself that some inspiration would strike when this meeting took place, and now she experienced that calm that comes when a maddening tangle of twine is finally resolved by a pair of shears. She focused on Normand's hands, clasped around the rim of a plate. His nails were filed smooth, one finger heavy under an unfamiliar ring. Irene lifted her eyes to his face, still not sure what she would do, but the expression that confronted her was so pinched, so comical in its self-important wariness, that she surprised even herself. She laughed, and that unaccustomed sound resembled, to those within earshot, nothing so much as the single, agitated bark of a large dog.

IN HER RUSH TO GET TO THE PARTY before Normand, Irene had left her kitchen in chaos, and now was incapable of postponing the mess until morning. She used the tip of a dinner knife to pry dried batter from the stainless steel mixing heads. She scoured long-standing stains from the copper bottom of each saucepan. She wiped down the doors of every oak cabinet and sprayed Glass Wax on the fixtures of the sink, the knobs of the stove. She used a toothpick to clear the holes of the salt and pepper shakers, and reorganized the spices in their proper alphabetical order. She swept and mopped the floor and stood still in a corner until it had dried. Then, moving to the living room, she dismantled the Christmas tree, wrapping each individual ornament in a paper towel, winding the strings of lights around her hand like bandages, vacuuming silver icicles from the carpet.

When she prepared for bed, Irene removed her wedding ring as usual to wash her face, but then hesitated to put it back on. It rested on the pale pink porcelain of her sink, its tiny diamond drinking in the glow of the vanity's illuminated frame. She had an urge to brush it into the drain, to send it through the septic system, to cause to happen by angry intent what she had often worried might occur through accident. It was an exciting temptation, but finally too extravagant. Instead, she let the ring be, turned off the light, and went to bed.

NORMAND SAT ALONE IN MARILYN'S living room drinking a cup of flat champagne, purchased as a symbol of brave defiance and popped when it had still seemed that the coming of a new year might be an occasion worth celebrating. He yearned to spike the champagne with something stronger, something with a kick to it, but didn't know Marilyn well enough, after all, to ask if she kept such a thing on hand. On the table, in a crumbled heap of tissue paper, was the sheer black nightgown he had bought by mistake one size too small.

Marilyn walked into the room, halfway into a debate with herself. "Am I right or am I right?"

"About what?" Normand didn't know whether to shake his head or nod. Irene had never required that he produce an opinion on command.

Marilyn exhaled in irritation. Then, noticing Normand's drink, she pulled herself together.

"We should use crystal," she decided, sliding the beveled door of a cherry hutch and finding two wineglasses. She wiped them hard with the hem of her dress.

"You don't have anything stronger, would you?"

"Opened champagne won't keep." Marilyn lifted the magnum, covered the spout with her thumb, and shook it to reproduce the lost carbonation. "I'll make up Arthur's room."

"But my things are at home," Normand said slowly. "All I've got are the clothes on my back."

"And your truck. And me." She sat beside him, took his hand, and pressed the ring into his skin.

"Anything you need, I've got it. Razor? Arthur's is on the shelf in the medicine cabinet. Snowmobile suit? Back closet. A handmade sweater for every day of the week."

Marilyn released her grasp, sliced a piece of cheese, centered it on a cracker, bit, chewed and swallowed.

Normand felt suspended between the tug of important thoughts—yet too empty to concentrate. On the one hand, he sensed this was the last night Irene might still let him come home. On the other, if he did, she would hold a permanent advantage.

"Why Arthur's room?" Normand tried to sound like an actor in a movie, sexy and flirtatious. "What's wrong with yours?" He turned his eyes to Marilyn's face but found it closed.

She patted his leg and stood up. "I need a place to myself. This way if you want to read in bed you won't disturb me. I'll get your sheets." As she passed the couch Marilyn reached out a hand. Normand caught it midway above the coffee table, gave it a squeeze.

"Aren't you a lamb?" Marilyn shook him off and retrieved his gift, as she had intended to do all along. "Don't want to spill anything on this before I exchange it," she explained, not unkindly. "It's been a long day for everybody."

Normand knew that Marilyn was waiting for him to look up at her, but his head felt too heavy to raise.

ALONE AND FEELING THE CHAM-
pagne, Normand regarded the room. Arranged on the
mantel were a collection of sea shells, the smallest on
each end, two large conchs tilted toward each other in
the center. Directly below hung Marilyn's girlhood
stocking, filled with Christmas candy. A spray of plastic
mistletoe, dripping imitation berries the size and color
of mothballs, was positioned above the door. The head-
set of the white Princess telephone was banded with
red ribbon to suggest a candy cane. He placed it beside
his ear and dialed.

After three rings Irene lifted the receiver.

Whenever Normand and Irene had talked this late at
night before, it was with eyes closed, head to head in
their queen-size bed, and about topics like whether or
not the window was open. Now he had no context for
what he had to say, no landmarks.

"You read about fires, about plane crashes . . ."
The index finger of Normand's free hand worked its
way into the spiral of the telephone cord, a rung at a
time. He was surprised to hear the emotion housed in
his voice and wondered, objectively, what Irene would
make of it.

If Irene had answered in a tone either sad or commanding, Normand would have gone to her, though
with a sense of having sacrificed something valuable. If

she had been bitter, he would have called the whole thing quits. He heard, however, only an airy well, like the distant echo of the sea.

On EASTER SUNDAY, MARILYN AN-nounced to Normand that they shouldn't marry.

"But we've been living together for four months," he protested. "What will people say?"

"Nothing more than they've already said. Besides, they're getting used to things. And Irene might fight a divorce."

"Don't I make you happy?" Normand wanted to know. He sat at the kitchen table in his bathrobe. His hair, flat on his left side where he had slept on it and lumpy on his right, framed his unshaven face. He wore wool socks because Marilyn insisted on turning the heat down to fifty-five at night, and on her advice he ate his toast without butter to avoid calories.

Marilyn squeezed his forearm. "Don't sulk," she said. "You never found the door locked yet. Come on, get dressed."

"What for?"

"It's Easter. It's time we went to church." She en-joyed his amazed expression. "Remember church? Where people go on Sundays? I laid out one of Arthur's good suits. You might as well get some wear out of his clothes."

Normand raised his eyes to the ceiling. "You're a crazy woman, you know that? What do you think they're going to say if we show up in a pew together?"

"A little more than they'll say next week, probably. News is news until the next thing happens—I learned that when my husband left me. Besides, what are we doing that people don't watch on TV every afternoon of the week?"

"You're never satisfied."

Marilyn enjoyed this description of herself. Normand's frequent recognitions of her outrageous qualities caused her to forgive him his clutter, the bathroom noise, the radio music he liked to play, the sleeping late on clear mornings. There were times, though, that she found herself wishing that Irene still had the daily care of him, the cleanup chores, the small duties of praise and complaint, the silent dinners for two.

As SPRING PROGRESSED, IRENE followed the receding snow line with a spade and a trowel, planting the bulbs she had tricked into indoor bloom during the winter. Alone in the evenings, she spent hours diagramming a new flower garden, a project so central to her imagination that often while taking a temperature or billing a patient, she found herself silently comparing types of fertilizer or the juxtaposition of marigolds and mums. She read the fine print of seed catalogs and started labeled flats on tables set before every south-facing window. When germination occurred she was ruthless in her thinning, allowing no more than two seedlings in each square.

As soon as the ground softened she drove stakes into the dirt, stretched string in taut lines to mark rows, measured with a ruler the correct depth of each harrow. She made her bargain with the land: to follow every instruction precisely, to employ only the choicest manure, to excise any growth, no matter how decorative, that was not part of her design. In return she expected results, and in her mind's eye her garden was already blossoming, filled with bees, as it carpeted the hill adjacent to her house. She counted the seeds she planted so that she would know the exact number of shoots to which she was entitled. When a few failed to yield, she wrote irate notes to the nurseries from which they had been ordered, and received not only replacements but letters of apology, which she saved, smoothed flat in a manila folder.

The days lengthened, and she wasted less and less time indoors. On weeknights she changed her clothes, made a sandwich and carried it with her to the yard, snatching a bite now and then as she worked. More than once she was so preoccupied in her labors that she used the wrong hand and so found herself chewing a mouthful of weeds instead of bread and peanut butter. When that happened she spit out the greens, trimmed off and discarded their roots, and worked the rest back into the loam with her fork.

Occasionally neighbors, sometimes even strangers once the plants began to flower, would pause in their walks and call compliments, but if it was at all possible, Irene ignored them. She was her own primary audience and resented the observations of others. Gawkers were lazy, taking for free the benefit of her work. Their words were cheap, no better than the dead leaves and blown debris that she picked from the rows and stored in black plastic trash bags every morning.

The vegetables were healthy. Beans and peas climbed the fencing propped behind their row; tomato plants, studded with small yellow stars, were contained by individual wire supports, round and barred as jail cells; green peppers were spaced between slender stalks of corn; and all along the perimeter the strong, looped vines of potatoes protruded from within the centers of spare truck tires, filled with straw and kept moist. The perfume of newly cut alfalfa rode in the air. Irene inhaled, closed her eyes, saw amazing colors on the inside of her lids.

IT HAD REACHED THAT POINT IN autumn when winter has the stronger pull over summer, when packed speckled leaves line the roads in humped lines as perfect as if they had been molded with pectin. The season had been mild, no dampness in the air or the soil, and grass had been allowed to grow long so that it wouldn't die at the roots. The air smelled like the inside of a woodstove, ready for a fire to be lit. Mottled corn was nailed in ribbon-tied clumps on every house door, and in most yards only the pansies thrived after an early frost.

Normand had learned to savor this time of year above all others, the last days before snowy roads required his services through the night. He used it to build up sleep, to collect rest in his muscles the way small rodents hoard seeds in their cheeks. It was to this peace that his memory retreated during a blizzard, to this hatless, gloveless temperature, dry and still. He had spent a week on the snowplow's engine, had driven the back roads slowly, alert for soft shoulders or runoff ruts that might catch a wheel. Alone on these reconnaissance trips, Normand regarded himself as a professional, an expert who saw what ordinary men might miss, and when he identified a loose bed or an unsupported erosion, he congratulated his keen eye and forgave himself his sins.

True, he had done a terrible deed—left his wife and taken up with a divorced woman. As a result, however, he had discovered that he was a man of more facets than he'd ever suspected, a man worthy of contemplation.

Now Normand felt a need to put his affairs in order. The major stumbling point to this end was his sure conviction that Irene nurtured an interpretation of himself that differed greatly from his own. She had been strangely uncurious about his new life, but Normand suspected what she might be privately thinking, and found it unjust. Their years together should amount to more than the debts and canceled checks forwarded in shoe boxes when the taxes came due, and he yearned for his wife to acknowledge the value of their shared time. The least Normand could do was to talk to Irene as a friend.

THE GARDEN WAS A SHOCK OF FUSED color as Normand walked toward it. Its bounty in the late October afternoon was testament to meticulous care: plants shrouded with newspapers or cloth at night, daily watering, pruning two buds of every three mums that appeared. It dominated the hillside beside the house, so bright that Normand had to squint when he raised his eyes from the loose gravel on the road.

He spotted Irene, bowed low behind a row of orange dahlias. She was turned away from him, and the familiar cast of her broad back and squared hips caused him to halt at the beginning of the walk.

"Working hard?"

Irene acted as though she didn't hear, so Normand tried a more direct approach.

"You probably wonder why I haven't mentioned divorce."

He was sure he heard a sharp intake of breath, so he didn't pause.

"I don't see the point of rushing it, you know? Where's the fire? Unless you need your freedom. Unless *you* want to sue for it."

Normand took the silence to mean no, and went on talking.

"You wouldn't know me anymore. Probably wouldn't want me back if you did."

He listened to his own words, startled by the reaction they provoked in him. The ache.

"If you do, say the word."

In the roar of silence that followed, there was nothing for Normand to do but look closely at what was all around him. So he stared at the four sapling maples he had planted in the front yard two years ago, their trunks now wrapped in gray burlap, secured by wire. He noticed that the stream rocks he had hauled for a border, then matched for size, needed fresh whitewash. He wanted more than anything to recross the line onto his own land, but Irene was like a bunker set into the ground. She was looking back at him calmly, and though inside he felt himself falling toward her, straining, straining through the air, without her invitation he couldn't move at all.

NAME
GAMES

"SHIRLEY-SHIRLEY BO-BERLEY banana-fana, fe-ferley, fee-fi mo merley: *Shirley!*"

"Yes," I answered as I awoke, which is strange because my name is Alex. I thought perhaps I had received a message from a former life and tried to concentrate hard on nothing so that I could recapture my Shirley existence, but I was not receiving. It was very early in the morning, so there was probably too much psychic static, the way sometimes you can't tune in even a nearby AM radio station because signals from Wheeling, West Virginia, or Chicago, Illinois, keep flickering off and on. You have to wait until the sun comes up. Somehow that quiets all the interference, but I don't know how. I tried to focus on that question, to visualize it. Noel believes that's the solution to problems of unclear conceptualization.

I shut my eyes and saw a horizon with little zigzagging lightning bolts, like from the RKO tower in old news cavalcades, trying to sneak around the sides. When the sun appeared, they fell as black streams of acid rain on the brightly lit fields of growing corn just shy of the earth's tilt.

I put on my terrycloth robe and went into the living room, where Noel was sleeping on the divan because last night he had been too annoyed with me to share a bed. The evening had started out fine, though I should have sensed hostility when he used his key instead of knocking. His flight from Dallas had been half empty, and those passengers who demanded refills of coffee or Bloody Marys had, for the most part, been seated on the aisle. Noel had not aggravated the sensitive muscles in his lumbar region by having to bend too often or too extensively from the waist, and as a result, he didn't need to lie on the floor for an hour, as he usually did after a long day, with the special Oriental wooden dowel braced beneath the small of his back.

"What's for dinner I'm starved," he said in one

breath. He refused to eat airline food, even the fruit plate.

"You have a selection: soy burger patties, eggs, trail mix, tofu, cheese corn puffs, mushrooms, Triscuits. Take your pick." I did not mention the single Le Menu Veal Parmigiana dinner, my personal favorite, which I had wrapped in aluminum foil and labeled "Bones for stock" before putting it in the rear of the freezer.

"It's cold here after Texas," Noel complained. "Do we have any ramen noodles?"

He opened the cabinet and began to move cans, dry pasta, bottles of herbs, then he froze.

"What, may I ask, is *this?*" He turned toward where I was seated in front of the TV. He held out, as though it were red dye #2, an unopened economy box of Duz detergent.

"You get a free tumbler inside," I explained.

"Well, I hope you *enjoy* it." He slammed the box on the counter in disgust, went into the bathroom and locked the door. We'd had this argument before but I had eliminated it from my mind during a recent purge of negative thoughts. Now it came back: Noel prides himself on product loyalty. He came from an All-Temperature Cheer–using family, and reasoned that if a soap had done a good job on clothes, year after year, it deserved continued support.

When Noel finally came out of the bathroom, his

face was grim. He answered my questions in monosyllabic words as he stood browsing the refrigerator and picked at a handful of trail mix. No, he didn't have an early call tomorrow. Yes, his co-worker Sandra had broken up with her husband. No, he didn't want me to run down to the store and get him his noodles.

All the chairs in the living room pointed toward the television, so he couldn't sit without seeming to join me for the end of *Starman,* but he did close his eyes. Eventually he put his fists over his ears as well and began to breathe deeply through his mouth, so I surrendered and turned off the videotape before its conclusion.

The instant I left the room to brush my teeth he made up the couch with the single one-hundred-percent goosedown bed pillow and the afghan from his mother, and by the time I had gargled, he was pretending to be asleep without saying good night.

I'm no stranger to Noel's moods, so I let him be, which I knew drove him crazy. I hummed to myself too, but not so loud that he could claim I did it to annoy him. I left the bedroom door slightly ajar, let the light spill out, and took a long time with my stretching exercises. I even wrote a nice newsy letter to my sister Bets, chuckling aloud at some of the more amusing lines, before setting the alarm and switching off the lamp. Then I called, in a pleasant voice, "Night, Noel." From the other room I heard him punch the pillow and roll over, but of course he didn't respond.

I HOPED THAT NOEL WAS READY TO make peace this morning because I was anxious to ask his opinion about the emergence of "The Name Game" from my subconscious. I tiptoed to the refrigerator, took the half-filled bag of Colombian-blend beans out of the freezer, and shook a scoopful into the electric grinder. Every noise magnified in the quiet apartment, and at the sound of the whir, Noel opened his eyes. We stared at each other, our expressions carefully neutral, while he decided on his attitude. I put a whole-wheat croissant into the toaster oven, poured the ground coffee into a Melitta filter, and added hot water up to the brim.

One of us had to take the risk. I carried two glasses of grapefruit juice to the couch and was relieved when, after a pause, Noel shifted his legs to make room for me. That was definitely a good sign, so I put his glass on the end table and told him about my Name Game dream. He swirled the juice around in his mouth, swallowed, wiped the ring of moisture from the table with the end of his afghan.

"Former life?" I suggested.

"You've got Shirley MacLaine on the brain," he said. That was a cheap shot, a remark not worthy of a person who was open to reaching for new possibilities.

"Your concern is deeply appreciated."

"Wasn't 'Shirley' the name in the original song?" Noel punched at my legs with his feet in apology. "Maybe it's as simple as you're just remembering the words the way they were written down."

"Even so . . ." He could be right about the lyrics, but I was reluctant to abandon what might be a rare subconscious clue to my psychic identity. Noel knew I was fascinated to think of history unfurling backwards in an interlocking chain of yins and yangs, males and females, with us along for the ride. The disappointment must have shown on my face.

"On the other hand," he said, "maybe it's more than that." He drew up his legs further, and I leaned against his hip. He reached to brush the hair away from my forehead. "You think we knew each other when you were a Shirley?"

"Without a doubt." Noel and I are cosmic twins, which is what has kept us together through all our arguments and crises. Our adviser, a gray-haired woman named Alicia whom we swear by, uncovered this amazing kinship the first time we visited her, when we were trying to decide if Noel should move in. Alicia immediately noticed that our left palms each had islands in

Venus, which is very unusual, and that was only the first indication of our bond. A few months later, Noel had cashed in his accumulated mileage to get me a pass on an international flight he was working, and we spent a weekend layover in Amsterdam. On the Sunday, walking hand in hand along a canal, we suddenly stopped and looked out at the water in silence. It was a heavy, overcast day, somewhat chilly. A wind from the North Sea made waves against the stone embankment, and I thought how depressing it was that our getaway couldn't last forever. I looked at Noel and his eyes were bright and troubled.

"I just experienced this positive tsunami of sadness," he said, echoing my emotion.

Later we recounted our thoughts to Alicia and she explained that Noel and I may once have been Dutch and lived together—as brother and sister, father and son, lovers, who knew?—in a house on that exact street, which was why those feelings of being where we belonged had washed over us.

"Who was the brother and who was the sister?" I wondered aloud, but Alicia, after studying our auras, could not tell.

"What did we do for a living?" Noel wanted to know. He was always thinking about quitting his flight attendant's job, despite its travel advantages and insurance benefits.

"I see one of you as a merchant," Alicia decided. Because she was from Ireland, she often used words that sounded old fashioned: "cobblers" fixed shoes and "tinkers" sold Avon door-to-door.

I LEANED AGAINST NOEL, RESTING my cheek on the rough wool of the afghan.

We both started to say something, almost in synch, and I laughed. More and more often it happened that our minds simultaneously hit on the same idea. I'd be thinking of Noel and he'd telephone from wherever he was, or I would have prepared precisely what he wanted for dinner. Alicia called this our "harmonizing."

"You first," I invited, feeling forgiven about the Duz and therefore generous.

Noel took a deep breath, let it out, and swung his feet to the floor. He drew the cover around his body and rested his elbows on his knees. I sensed conflict, and put my hand on his back to show support.

"You know Sandra?" he asked the floor.

I nodded. Noel became emotionally involved with the personal problems of his fellow attendants, took their worries to heart.

"Well, she left him, her husband."

"I'm sure it's for the best," I said. "You said she wasn't happy."

"Alex, she left him for me."

There are moments in life when time freezes, or at least goes into slow motion. My hand was glued to Noel's back and nothing would make it move. The cooling element in the refrigerator clattered and when it stopped the silence was so absolute that from the bedroom I could hear a click as the numbers changed on my clock radio.

"I'm going to try it," he went on at last. "I have to know."

I heard him, understood the spoken words, but all I could think of was my hand. How heavy it had become, how useless. If I managed to lift it from the rise and fall of Noel's breath, where would I find to set it down?

GROOM
SERVICE

1.

"S HE'S A PIECE OF PURE QUARTZ,"
Bernard's mother, Martha, said to Marie's mother,
Blanche. "A one-in-a-million that you find after walking the beach for half your life with your eyes on the
ground. If I had a child like that I would keep her in a
safe place."

Blanche paused her blade midway down the side of
the fish she was scaling. Her face betrayed no expression except exertion, and even in this intermission her
teeth remained set, flexing her jaw. The trader steel

reflected what little light filtered through the planks of the smokehouse, and the confined air still smelled green. Blanche had hewn the boards with a mallet and chisel in May, as soon as the ground firmed from the spring runoff, and it took a while before the scent of fire crowded that of drying wood. With her broad thumb she flicked a piece of fin off the carved knife handle, then continued her motion.

Martha waited. She had all the time it took.

"You don't know," said Blanche. She shook her head as if its secrets rolled like line-weights from side to side. She drew a heavy breath. "You can't imagine. You with such a boy."

Martha sat straighter, all ears, while her hands continued to explore, repairing the tears on the net that lay across her lap and hid her pants and boots. Her fingers moved automatically, finding holes, locating the ends of broken cord and twisting them into square knots. She kept her nails sharp and jagged, and when they weren't enough, she bowed her head and bit off any useless pieces. This was mindless work, the labor of ten thousand days, and could be done as easily in the dark as in the light. It required no involvement. Her thoughts were elsewhere.

"You mean Bernard?" Her voice was wary. She had three sons and needed to be sure she knew the one Blanche had in mind.

"Ber-*nard*," Blanche nodded, giving the knife a last run, then inspecting the fish closely before tossing it into the large basket at her feet. The water slopped onto the floor and, from there, leaked to the shale ground inches below. Blanche arched her back and massaged her spine with her fist. With her other hand she reached for the cup of cooled tea that she had nursed for the past half-hour. Martha let the net rest and joined her.

"People talk about him, you know," Blanche said. "His looks, that goes without saying, but the other things too. The respect he pays the old folks. His singing. His calmness. His hunting skill. You must be proud."

Martha closed her eyes as if in great pain. "He is my punishment," she confessed, "but I don't know what I could have done so terrible as to deserve him. He stays out until morning. His hair is always tangled. I sometimes think that the game he brings home has died before he found it, the meat is so tough. You must have him confused with another boy. Or perhaps, with a girl like Marie, you find it hard to think ill of any child."

"Now you make fun of me," Blanche said. "It is well known that Marie has turned out badly. She is lazy and disrespectful, conceited and stubborn. I try my best to teach her, and so do my sisters and even my mother, but she folds her arms and stares at nothing. Hopeless.

And she will never find a husband. A boy's mother would have to be desperate to send her son courting at my house."

"But not as desperate as the mother who could tolerate the thought of Bernard as a son-in-law," Martha said. "That would be true desperation. I will never be free of him. I will grow old with him at my side, and with no granddaughters or grandsons to comfort me."

"If only someone like your Bernard would find an interest in Marie," Blanche said as if she had not heard Martha. "If only some young man exactly like him would consent to live in my house, how I would welcome him. I would treat him as my own blood."

The two women met each other's gaze at last. Each held a cup to her lips, and after a few seconds, each drank. Each replaced her cup on the table between them. Each held her mouth firm. Blanche found her knife and reached for a new fish, cool and slippery as a stone over which much water has rushed. Martha shifted the net in her lap, moving a new section to the center. The smell of salt rose like steam as her hands went to work.

"I will speak to him," Martha said.

"And I to her," Blanche replied. "But I know her answer already. I have seen how she regards him."

"She will not be disappointed." Martha allowed one wave of pride to crest. "He's not so bad."

Blanche glanced up at Martha, then looked quickly back to her work. Bernard must be good indeed, she thought, if Martha could not better contain herself.

2.

Bernard was drawing with charcoal on a piece of driftwood when his mother returned home. He was twenty-two, lean, and had large teeth. His eyes were dark beneath unusually thick brows, and his hands were long and broad. At the sound of Martha's step, he jumped to his feet and assumed the air of a person about to do something important. His fingers curved as if to hold a tool or a weapon and his eyes narrowed as if to see something far away. He was busy at nothing, his energy humming, ready for a focus. But for once she made no comment about his sloth. She did not despair at the time he wasted scratching on any smooth surface. She did not inspect his sketch and then toss it into the cooking fire. In fact, this afternoon she dealt with him rather mildly.

"Well, it's arranged," she announced. "I spent an endless morning with your future mother-in-law and before I left she had agreed to let you come to see Marie. Don't think it was easy."

Bernard's eyes followed his mother's movements as she crossed the floor and sat in exhaustion on the bed.

She pushed off her boots, still caked with beach mud, and rubbed her feet together. She wore no socks.

"Marie?" he said at last. "She's too young. You should have asked me first."

Martha's glare clapped a hand over his mouth. In a moment, Bernard tried again.

"I know they're a good family. I know you want to do right for me. But you could . . . *we* could have discussed this. I mean, I think of her as a little girl, not a *wife.*" The word, a stranger on Bernard's tongue, vibrated in the air.

"Stop whining." Martha lost patience. "Who do you 'think of' as a wife? *Doris?*"

Bernard blushed. He wasn't surprised that his mother knew about him and Doris, but it did not seem fair for her to mention it. Doris was a widow whose name brought nervous laughs to teenage boys and smiles of disapproval to everyone else. She was a woman almost twice Bernard's age with a missing front tooth and eyes that sparked in his memory, a woman who had summoned him for an errand six months ago and whom he now loved better than he would have thought possible. But it was true: he had never thought of Doris as a wife.

"You should see yourself," Martha said. "Keep that face and you won't have to worry about marrying anyone. But don't expect me to support you forever." She noticed the driftwood, still on the floor, and nudged it with her toe to get a better view. Bernard had outlined the mountain across the bay from the village, and tucked a large sun behind its peak. When he drew it he thought it was his best work, but now its lines looked smudged and shaky. Martha leaned forward to pick it up and turn it over, as if expecting another illustration on the back. Finding none, she held it out for Bernard to take.

"Give this to your Doris," she said. "It looks like her under the blanket where she spends her time."

Bernard didn't move, but he watched the wood until his mother let it fall to the floor. He was angry at the shame he felt. He was angry that he knew it was just a matter of time until he would have to call on Marie. He was angry that his mother was right: his mountain *did* look like Doris, turned on her side.

3.

When Blanche went into the house and told Marie that their problems were over, that Bernard, the catch of the village, would be courting, she expected some reaction, but her daughter simply folded her arms and stared at the fire.

"Don't you hear me?" Blanche demanded. "Bernard. Coming to see you. Can't you be happy? Can't you say something?"

Marie, however, only rolled her eyes and drummed her fingers against the pine bench upon which she sat. She wore a close-knit woven cap that, in combination with her unfortunately weak chin, made her head resemble an acorn. She was fifteen, just out of her confinement, trained for adulthood to the limits of Blanche and her sister's patience, but still a sulking child. At length she drew up her knees, circled them with her arms, and watched her mother from the corner of her eye.

Blanche stood across the long room, talking to her older sister Bonnie. She was not hard to overhear.

"Does she say 'thank you'? Does she appreciate what it means to her, to all of us, to get that damn Martha to agree? Does she care that Bernard could have any girl, from any family?"

Bonnie shook her head sadly. Her surviving children had all been boys and had long since moved to the houses of their wives' families, so she had no experience with reluctant girls, unless, she thought, she counted her memories of Blanche. But that would not do to say, especially not in earshot of Marie, who sat with her head cocked in their direction. Blanche's daughter was the hope of the next generation, the one who had to bring in a husband and produce more daughters than her mother or aunt, if the family was to regain its position. For a moment Bonnie thought of suggesting to Blanche that they present that information to Marie directly, to drop the shadows and point out both her responsibility and her power, but then she rejected the idea. The girl was impressed enough with herself as it was. Instead, Bonnie sympathized with her sister and cast occasional looks at her niece in hopes of catching on Marie's face a secret, a streak of pleasure.

4.

"What am I supposed to do?" Bernard asked the next time his uncle visited. Bernard had waited for a private moment, and it came when, just before sleep, Theodore had stepped outside to relieve himself. The trees around the village seemed closer at night, taller, like the sides of a box.

From the darkness came rattling sounds of strangulation that Bernard eventually identified as the older man's yawn. When it, and the noise of splashing water, had abated, Theodore spoke. It was clear that he understood Bernard's problem.

"You do whatever they tell you and you hope they're not as bad as they could be," Theodore said. "You don't complain. You don't assume anything. You stay out of the way, because you never know what they're going to find to dislike. You be what they want."

"It's not fair." Bernard leaned against the side of the house and searched the sky. Thin clouds, silver as wet spiderwebs, passed in the night wind.

"That's true, but there are other things in the world besides owning real estate. Your true home will remain here at your mother's, just as it has been for me, but you can't *live* here forever. You need independence, distance, the chance to be a man in a place where you were never a boy. Once you get yourself established, you'll understand what I mean. Your life is not all in-doors. You'll hang around with your brothers-in-law, your uncles, your friends. Spend time at the men's house. Go to the sweat bath and gripe, or listen to the complaints of others and make jokes. In a year all your wife's family will care about is whether or not you bring in your share. By then you'll know what's what."

"But what if I don't get along with Marie?"

"Do get along with her. Get along with her mother. Get along with her auntie. But on your own time do what you want. It's not a big price to pay. It's a daughter-poor clan and the one they've picked out for you is going to control everything someday: rich fish-ing sites, a big house. Behave yourself now and you'll get your reward. It's not like you're marrying a youn-gest sister with no prospects."

Which was, Bernard knew, what had happened

to Theodore. No wonder he was not more sympathetic.

"How do I tell Doris?" Bernard asked. This was something he had struggled with for days.

"Doris! She could have told *you*. It's good news to her. She gets a younger guy, fresh the way she likes them, and no hard feelings between you." Theodore laughed, and put an arm around Bernard's shoulders. "Listen to some advice, from your great-uncle through me to you," he said. "Groom service is the worst part, so make it as short as possible. Convince her family you won't be a pain in the ass to live with. Rule number one: appreciate everything they do. Compliment, compliment, compliment."

"Did you do that?" Bernard asked. "Did my mother's husband do that?"

"Do fish fry in hot grease? But don't take my word for it. Ask Pete. He's your father."

"I'd be embarrassed," Bernard said. "He and I never talk about serious matters. He's not of the clan."

"A man's a man," Theodore said.

5.

"This is what you do," Martha instructed.

It was not yet light and she had awakened Bernard

from a sound sleep. He blew into a cup of hot tea as he listened, let the darkness hide the resentment in his face.

"You go hunting and you catch something *good,* I don't care what. Something a little unusual. A beaver, maybe, or a goose. *Not* something small and easy. *Not* a squirrel. *Not* fish. You bring it home and I'll help you clean it. You leave a portion for me as if that's what you always do, to help provide for your family, but you take the best part and you set yourself in front of Blanche's door. You only speak if you're spoken to. You wait for *them* to ask *you.* And if they don't, which they won't right away, you act unconcerned. You do this every day until they invite you in, and then I'll tell you what to do next. This is your chance, so don't ruin it. Now move."

Bernard stepped out into the chill morning grayness, thought briefly of visiting Doris before he went hunting, but then abandoned the idea. He had heard through his mother's husband that Doris had made friends with a seventeen-year-old boy named James.

The dew from high grass had soaked through to Bernard's feet before he reached the edge of the woods. He realized his mother had forgotten to feed him breakfast, forgotten to make him a lunch. He heard a duck call from the lake and paused, but then continued on. He could hear his mother in his mind, and she said a duck wouldn't do.

6.

"He's *there!*" Bonnie dropped the firewood she was carrying and rushed to Blanche's side.

Her sister was stirring a pot on the fire, as if what it contained were all that concerned her. "I have eyes," Blanche said. "Keep your voice down. He'll hear you."

"Did you see what he had?" Bonnie asked. "I got a glimpse of something flat and dark, but I didn't want him to catch me looking."

"I think it was a beaver tail. Would you believe, he had the nerve to hold it up to me and smile the first time I passed."

"No!"

"I thought he was better trained. It simply means he'll have to wait longer."

"Did Marie see him yet?"

"She won't go outside." Both sisters turned to the gloom in the rear of the room where Marie crouched, her head lowered over a stick game. Her long hair was loose and covered her shoulders like a shawl, her back to the doorway.

7.

"Well, what happened?" Martha demanded when Bernard returned home late in the evening.

"Nothing happened," Bernard said, and threw himself down on his blankets. He raised an arm to cover his eyes, then turned to face the wall.

Martha spotted the sack her son had dropped on the floor and looked inside. The beaver tail and quarters were exactly as she had cleaned them that afternoon, and she took them out to add to the broth she had prepared.

"At least we'll eat well for a while," she said.

"I'm not hungry," Bernard replied, but his mother ignored him.

"Tell me everything."

"There's nothing to tell. I walked over there, dressed like I was going to a feast, carrying that beaver. I trapped it clean, surprised it so completely, there wasn't even adrenaline in its flesh. I thought they'd taste it, invite me to supper, but they walked by me like I wasn't there, their noses in the air."

"Whose noses?" Martha wanted to know.

"The mother and the aunt."

"Not the girl?"

"I saw no girl. I heard no girl."

"Ah," said Martha. "So she's shy. Good."

"Why good?"

"Because then she won't bully you at first, stupid boy. I've seen what happens to the husbands of the bold ones."

The smell of stewing meat filled the room, warm, rich, brown. Martha's husband Pete came into the house at the scent, tipped his head in his son's direction, and asked, "Hard day?"

8.

For a week, then two weeks, the same pattern was repeated. Only the animals changed: they ranged from a porcupine to a hind quarter of caribou, from a fat grouse on a bad day to a string of matched silver salmon on a good one. Once Bernard thought he saw a black bear dive into the brush at the side of a stream, but he was momentarily afraid to investigate, and later berated himself. With a bear skin, he thought too late, he would have been irresistible and his long afternoons and evenings at Blanche's closed door would have been over.

As a month passed, Bernard gave up hope. He lost the alertness he had once felt when Blanche or Bonnie or Marie, the most unsympathetic of them all, approached, and he soon tired of the commiseration that Blanche's and Bonnie's husbands cast in his direction as they went about their business. They could remember, their expressions said, what it was like to wait outside this house, but there was nothing they could do. A word from them might slow the process rather than speed it up, might do more damage than good. If boredom was patience, Bernard achieved patience. If learning to exist without expectation of fulfillment was maturity, Bernard matured. At first he used his time to remember Doris, to wonder what she was doing and to regret not doing it with her. Later he thought about hunting, how he could have succeeded the times he had failed, how the animals behaved, how they smelled and sounded. Finally he found himself thinking about Pete, his father, in different ways than he ever had before. In Bernard's mind Pete became more than just his mother's husband; he became another man, an earlier version of Bernard, a fellow sufferer. It had not previously occurred to Bernard how hard it was to be forever a stranger in the house where you lived, to be always a half-visitor. He wondered how Pete stayed so cheerful, and wondered if his grandmother had kept his father waiting long at the doorway before inviting him inside. On an afternoon late in the second week, Bernard had a thought so profound, so unprecedented, that it straightened his back. What if, he wondered, his grandmother had not let Pete in at all? What if Pete had been judged inadequate? Where would that have left Bernard?

The next morning when he went hunting, Bernard returned to the place where he had seen the bear, hid himself behind a log, and waited.

9.

"Did you hear?" Pete asked Theodore as they walked the trail from the sweat bath to their wives' houses.

"About Bernard's bear?"

"It must have weighed three hundred pounds. I didn't know Bernard had it in him."

"Have you forgotten what sitting in front of a house will drive you to? What did you catch to get inside Blanche's?"

"Nothing," Pete said. "It was me she couldn't resist."

"You forget," Theodore replied. "I was still a boy in that house. I recall their words of you. Let me see . . . I seem to remember some mention of the small size of certain of your parts."

"Poor brother-in-law," Pete said. "You still don't realize the lengths to which they went to avoid hurting your feelings! And how *is* your wife? How is the health of her many elder sisters? Is it true that they become stronger and more robust with every year?"

10.

On the second day of the fifth week, just as she passed through the door, Blanche reached down her right hand and snagged one of the bear claws that rested in the basket by Bernard's leg. So quick was her movement, so apparently disconnected to the intent of her mind, so complete her distraction, that Bernard had to look twice to make sure it was gone. All the same, he felt a warm flush spread beneath the skin of his neck, and a feeling of inordinate pride suffused him so thoroughly that he had difficulty remaining still. He had been found worthy, and now it was only a matter of time.

Every day, with more pause and deliberation, Blanche browsed through his offerings and always selected some choice token. Her expression betrayed no gratitude, yet Bernard was sure that occasionally she was pleasantly surprised. Afraid to unbalance their precarious arrangement, he sat still as a listening hare in her presence. He kept his eyes lowered and held his breath until she had departed, but remained ever watchful for any cue that his probation had progressed. At last it came.

"Bernard!" Blanche said one day. She stood in the doorway, her hands on her hips, her head cocked to the side in amazement. "Is that you crouching there so quietly? Please, come in and share our supper, poor as it is. What a pleasure to see you."

Bernard rose slowly, stiff in his joints and half-skeptical that this was some joke, some new test, but when he entered the house, Blanche's hospitality continued and was joined by that of Bonnie, who sat by the fire trimming her husband's hair with a squeaking scissors. "Sit, sit," she motioned to a bench near the door. "What a shy boy you are. Luckily we have some nice moose to feed you."

Indeed they did. Bernard recognized the remains of the foreleg he had offered yesterday. Bonnie passed him a plate with a small portion of tough gristle, gray and cooled. He knew what to say.

"This is wonderful," he exclaimed. "The best I've ever tasted. What cooks you are. But you are too generous. Let me put some back in the pot."

When they refused, politely and with many denials of his compliments, Bernard made a great show of eating. The act of digestion absorbed his total concentration. He rubbed his stomach and cast his eyes to the ceiling in delight. With great subtlety he periodically raised his hand to his mouth, as if to wipe some grease, and used that motion to conceal the small bits of undigestible food he removed from his cheeks and tucked secretly into his pockets.

When he finished, Bernard sat nervously, breathless with anxiety. From the corner of the room he detected a space so devoid of movement that it attracted his attention. He looked, then quickly looked away. Yet his eyes still registered the image of Marie, her hair oiled and braided, wearing a new dress and a necklace made of bear claws, sitting as composed and shaded as a perfect charcoal sketch.

11.

"You know, Pete," Martha said as she lay by her husband's side under a robe, "watching Bernard lately brings back memories."

"To me too. Your mother was a terror."

"I notice you still whisper such words, even though she's more than four years gone."

Pete shifted his position and propped on an elbow. In the moonlight Martha's face was seamless and young. A beam like the hottest part of a coal danced off her dark eye. He ran his fingers along her cheek and she turned her head in comfort. "You look the same as then," he said.

Martha caught his hand and brought it to her mouth, let it feel the smile.

"I pestered her, you know, to let you in," she said. "You didn't care."

"I didn't care the day you found the eagle feathers? I didn't care the day you came an hour later than always?"

"It was raining," Pete said. "The ground was soft

and I kept sinking to my knees. I couldn't arrive at your door covered in mud."

"I thought you weren't coming. I confronted my mother and told her that her slowness had cost me . . ."

"Cost you what?" Pete asked, when Martha's silence persisted.

"Enough talk."

12.

Marie watched the back of Bernard's head and admired the sleek sheen of his long hair, the play of muscles in his arms at his every movement. During the last month she had studied every part of him so completely that she could create him in her imagination whenever she chose, and lately she chose often. She had to fight not to laugh when they gave him the worst meat and he had to spit into his hand and act as though it were delicious. She watched the way his fingers held the plate, the way he sat so compact and attentive. She waited for the sound of his soft voice and wondered what he would say when he could speak in private. She made a game of observing his eyes until just the second before they turned to her, and believed she had been discovered only once.

13.

Bernard ate almost all of his meals at Blanche's house now, and gradually became more relaxed. For one thing, his distribution increased in both quality and quantity, and he could now expect a reasonable piece of meat or salmon. For another, Blanche's and Bonnie's husbands had begun to join him on his hunts, to show him places to fish that only members of this household knew. He found he liked these men and began to call them "uncle."

Blanche herself still frightened him, but not all the time. There were moments when he found approval in her gaze, times when some word of hers sounded almost like a joke. Bonnie was warmer, more solicitous of his needs, more delighted at the food he brought, and Bernard regarded her as an ally.

As far as Marie was concerned, he still had no clue to her feelings. Even Pete and Theodore observed that this game was lasting longer than the usual and debated whether something might be wrong. They were full of advice for Bernard, full of ideas of how to please Marie, full of reminders that it was her agreement, more than anyone's, that was necessary. But no matter what Bernard did, Marie would not look at him or give him any sign of encouragement. He grew despondent, lost his appetite, found himself thinking once again of Doris and the ease of their association. Marie seemed totally beyond his reach, the focus of mystery and impossible desire. And so he was unprepared on the night, just before the first frost of winter, when, with shaking hands, Marie herself passed him a plate of food.

"This is for you," she said so softly he could barely hear, and she sat beside him while, slowly and with great emotion, he ate.

14.

A year later, while waiting for the birth of Marie's first child, Blanche and Martha passed the time by nibbling strips of dried eel. Martha, who had no love for the oily skin, threw hers into the fire, where it sizzled briefly.

"The midwife predicts a girl," Blanche said. "When she spun the charm above Marie's stomach, it revolved to the left."

"A girl is most rewarding," Martha nodded. "But there is a special satisfaction in raising boys. So often I think of times when Bernard was young, so often I miss him around the house."

Blanche reached for another stick of *baleek* and did not answer. Her silence was immediately noticed, as she knew it would be.

"How is he doing?" Martha asked at last.

"He will learn," Blanche said. "He has potential. It is clear he cares greatly for Marie, and she is patient."

"That is one word for it." Martha tossed a handful of scraps into the flame and watched the light flare and dance. "Of course, Bernard was used to . . ." She shifted her weight, cleared her throat. "He had such a *happy* home that I'm sure it has taken some adjusting on his part in new surroundings."

"Yes, he *was* somewhat spoiled. But I think he has a good heart."

"As well he must, to remain loyal to such a chinless girl."

"One only hopes their child will inherit the mother's disposition and not be sulky and resentful of every request."

"One can but pray it will have the father's looks and personality."

A single rope of eel remained on the plate. Both women extended a hand toward it, hesitated, and withdrew. It rested between them as they cleaned their teeth with fine bone picks, carefully wiped their fingers, and when, at the sound of Marie's first muffled protest, they rose together and rushed to her side, it remained behind.

ANYTHING

I T WAS ROMANTIC HOW GEORGE proposed to me six months after we broke up, and after I was already formally engaged to a man I didn't love.

I had found myself between too many things—jobs, boyfriends, apartments—and so started going out with Alan even though he wasn't especially my type. I didn't pretend with him either, so when on our fourth date he said he wanted to get married, I thought he was fooling around, reached over and pulled his ear. But he was sincere. I could tell because the ends of his mouth turned down in hurt while his chin rose in indignation.

"We don't like each other," I reminded him. "We're just a mutual convenience," quoting his own words to me of last week.

"We can learn," he answered, and made his eyes go glittery.

It would have been more trouble than it was worth to contradict him. He seemed so sure that I thought maybe he was right. No matter which way I added Alan up, his pluses always outweighed his minuses. Thinking about him reminded me of that game you play with your hands and fingers where paper covers rock, scissors cuts paper, rock breaks scissors. With Alan it was like dependable beats fun, rich tops poor, somebody is bound to be better than nobody.

Soon afterwards, the plans took on a life of their own. His mom handled the arrangements, asking only that I immediately provide her with a list of the ten couples, no singles, I wanted invited to the reception. Naturally, George was the first person who came to my mind, but he was impossible. Who would he escort as his date without making me jealous? However, I had to admit that he should hear the big news from me first. I also had to admit I wanted the satisfaction.

Three weeks previously, George, my bachelor number one, had accepted a deejay job during the drive-home slot on an easy-listening AM station in Bardstown, so I needed to get his mailing address from his mother. Alberta was too p.o.'d to ask what I wanted of him—she blamed me for her son moving downstate—and I didn't volunteer. I blamed her for George.

I flipped through the postcards on the rack at Taylor's, decided against the photo finish of a horse race at Churchill Downs, and finally selected a twilight aerial view that showed the three bridges that span the Ohio from Kentucky to Indiana. The skyscrapers made Louisville look like a big city, which I thought might make George consider all he had voluntarily given up by running away.

"Dear George, There's no easy way to tell you. August twenty-first is my wedding day. *This is no joke.* I hope you're as happy for me as I am. Fondly, Aileen."

I chose *fondly* after considering many alternatives: love, best wishes, warmly, your friend, yours truly, or nothing. Fondly sounded wistful, like a memory rather than a statement of fact, plus it wasn't cold. George deserved that much after our year together as a couple.

Two nights later, Alan invited me out for a meal and a movie, my pick, and I said Burger King just to see him roll his eyes while he wondered if I was for real. Besides, I liked the onion rings. We were sitting there, in the middle of reviewing our honeymoon itinerary—

we had firm reservations on a flight to San Antonio and a week's prepaid family pass to Five Flags Over Texas, a destination the travel agent assured us was still undiscovered—when one of the busboys tapped me on the shoulder.

"You Aileen?" he inquired.

I must have blinked.

"Because if you are you have an emergency phone call."

I looked at Alan and he raised his hands, palms up, as if to say, "Hey, don't blame me."

I followed the Burger King guy through the swinging doors to the back.

"How did you know I was me?" I asked him.

"They said look for a tall redhead eating onion rings."

There were three long metal tables, a row of built-in microwaves, a grill with burgers sizzling on it. An army of teenagers in green and white uniforms were building sandwiches, each one adding their particular item as the open bun halves were shipped down the line. They all stopped their work and stared as I walked by, but I pretended not to notice. The receiver of a wall phone was off the hook and resting on a little table.

"Hello?" I said, not knowing what to expect. Posted on the wall in front of me was a list of emergency numbers—police, fire, ambulance, poison center—and a set of illustrated instructions for giving the Heimlich Maneuver.

"It's George. Don't hang up. Something's happened to me."

The manager was listening to see if the crisis was bad enough to have summoned me behind the scenes. I could tell from his face that nothing short of death would satisfy him, so I clapped my hand to my cheek and turned away, wedging my forehead into the angle of the walls.

"What?" I whispered. Through the receiver I could hear Barbra Streisand singing "Stony End," so I assumed George was calling from work.

"You can't get married. You'll hate yourself. You can't be in love."

I was torn between smiling and slamming down the phone because as usual George had me figured too well, one of his more annoying habits.

"You want to know how I know?"

"How?" I admitted without meaning to. He sounded rushed, which probably meant a commercial was coming up and he would have to put me on hold. When we were first dating I used to find this habit exciting, as though whatever I said might inspire the next number George played. Then I found out that all his music came off a standard feed beamed from Costa Mesa, California, to a satellite and then to every subscribing station. George just had to fill in the gaps with local programming.

"Am I right?"

"You're crazy."

"Don't do it, Aileen. It would spell disaster. I'll be right back."

"Disaster!" I repeated very loud. I appeased the manager with the tone of my voice, and he turned away, suddenly bashful at my grief. When George returned, now with the Beach Boys in the background, I pressed my lips against the little holes in the mouthpiece for privacy. "What do you want from me?"

"Anything."

That may not sound like much to you, or maybe like too much. It didn't specifically include the words *love* or *marriage,* for instance, but it didn't exclude them, either. How much detail *can* you communicate over the telephone of a fast-food franchise during a single cut of an old song? Maybe it was the setting more than anything else that undecided me. Burger King is the kind of place where you either knew which options you preferred, or you got out of the line.

"Well," I said, stalling.

"Okay?" The song was "Cherish," which shouldn't have mattered.

WHEN I HUNG UP I KEPT MY HAND on the wall for a minute. I felt as though I had stepped off one of those carnival rides where you're strapped in a cage that arcs to the right while the floor tilts to the left and the whole deal spins around at top speed. Finally, I nodded to the manager, who was looking at the phone as though he expected the President of the United States to call at any second and say he had tried before but the line had been busy.

"I can't thank you enough," I said, then made my way through the doors and returned to our booth. Alan was pulling the last of his vanilla shake into his mouth through a straw. He lifted his eyebrows in a question as I sat down. I hated the way he never used words if he could move one of his body parts instead. I noticed that he had not been so concerned about my call as to wait for me. His Whopper was gone, along with exactly his half of our shared jumbo order of onion rings.

"That was George," I told him. "He wants me back and I said yes."

As I watched Alan react, I realized why it would have been a mistake to marry him. He set his cup on the table (alert concern), carefully wiped his mouth with a paper napkin (confused thought), and shook his head slowly (stunned disappointment). I waited him out, so at last he had to speak.

"I don't believe what I'm hearing, Aileen." His voice was stern, sure of itself.

I nodded, covered his hand with one of mine, and sighed. Two could play charades.

Alan had a bit of food stuck between his teeth. His hand lifted toward his chin but he saw me notice and caught himself. We both realized that he would lose his bid for sympathy if he revealed the existence of a thought unrelated to my announcement.

"So that's it? Just like that?" Irritation had crept into his tone and I could imagine all the complaints that were piling up in his brain, all the things that would have to be returned or canceled—or couldn't be canceled without penalty. All the excuses his mother would have to make. His eyes zeroed in on my ring finger, focusing on the diamond he had given me.

I took it off, polished it against my blouse, and set it neatly in the center of an onion ring.

He turned his head away and stared hard at the door, as though he expected Dan Rather to show up and put this news flash in perspective.

"Come on, Alan. You know they'll be lining up for you when the word gets out."

From the expression that gradually overtook his face, I could tell he conceded the point.

AFTER I GOT HOME I REMEMBERED that there were some critical bits of information missing from my immediate schedule, like what happened next. Was I supposed to call George, or should I wait to hear from him? His face rose in my memory, which was no help. George was one of those radio people who sounded better than he came across in person. His voice was pure "Entertainment Tonight" but his looks were average, medium everything: height, weight, coloring. When we were dating, sometimes I would close my eyes and just listen.

I didn't have George's unlisted home number in Bardstown, didn't know the call numbers of his station, and I didn't look forward to bothering Alberta again without offering an explanation. Still, the circumstances demanded some action on my part. The alternative brought to mind a book report I wrote in eleventh grade about an old lady who sat in her wedding dress for fifty years because the groom didn't show. The five-tiered cake got covered with cobwebs.

"You're home early." While I was sunk deep in worry my dad had materialized at the door of my room. He acted afraid I might bite his head off for noticing a fact about my life.

"Later than you think," I told him.

"You won't believe in a million years who called you."

"And you won't believe what he wanted." It occurred to me that if Dad had gotten Burger King confused with McDonald's, I might still be engaged to Alan.

"Which was?" Dad was pressing his luck, but for once I didn't resent him invading my privacy.

Just then the phone rang, and I jumped for it. Since it was after ten o'clock, it had to be one of my fiancés, past or present, heads or tails. It was George.

"I've been giving this a lot of thought," he said, as if a long time had passed since our last conversation. There was empty air behind him. His shift was over.

"I took your advice and broke up with Alan," I interrupted before he could give me the benefit of his conclusions. What record was playing in George's head, I wondered. What record was playing in mine? "The Boxer."

I watched Dad's eyes get curious. I shook my head, pointed for him to close the door after him. Once I was alone I turned my attention back to the telephone.

"Anybody home?"

George didn't seem as delighted as he should have been at my announcement. He didn't act as though "anything" was still what he wanted from me.

"Hey, George?" I asked him. "Why did you call me at the restaurant?"

He considered before he answered. "Actually I tried you at home first," he corrected.

There was something he wasn't telling me.

"Was it Emmylou Harris again?" I asked. One time when we had a fight "Together Again" came onto George's schedule just when he was in a weak moment, and he had called to apologize for whatever it was I was mad about, even though he later admitted that he didn't truly believe he was at fault. Music was an occupational hazard for him, which I could understand. Anyone can fall into one of those moods where every lyric sounds tailor-made and contains some great personal truth. The words speak to you, tell you what to think, what's supposed to happen next. In George's line of work, this was an ever-present danger. Some super-deejay in California could pull your strings, inhabit your body from outer space by remote control.

"No. It wasn't like that." George cleared his throat and went on. "Your dad gave me a hard time."

I could imagine Dad, turning the screws on George for disappointing me. "She's out to dinner with her *boyfriend*," he would have rubbed it in. He'd tell me all about it if I let him, and maybe I would.

"The question is," I thought out loud, "what did you have in mind to say in the first place?"

"Nothing specific," George answered, but then contradicted himself, just before breaking the connection. "I can't explain it over the phone."

This was not what I had hoped to hear, but it didn't surprise me. What I liked about George all along was how he would every once and a while surrender to his instincts, live up to his vocal cords, and when he got like that he was capable of saying a word like *anything,* and I'd believe in him. But this time was no different than others. Typically he had come down to earth, started thinking, gotten cagey and normal and into himself, and turned back into that same disappointment I had already put behind me. George was a man you could love in a crisis, in a frenzy, in a moment of truth. It was the other ninety-nine percent of the time that dealing with him was a problem for me. I spent so much of my life in a condition you might call general wishing—a perfect husband, wonderful children, a happy home life, a good job, financial security— that the concrete rarely measured up. It was as though each of my wants was a blank piece of paper, the name of a category pre-stamped across the top, and someday I would recognize the details to sketch in. That was what passed for success: a book of full-color pages.

I T   W A S   L A T E ,   B U T   T H I S   W A S   A   S P E -
cial circumstance. Alberta answered on the first ring.

"George, have you lost your mind?" she demanded
before I could speak.

"My sentiments exactly," I said, which threw her
off.

"I wasn't referring to what you imagine," Alberta
said, recognizing my voice instantly. "It was about
something else."

"Look, Alberta, this wasn't my idea. I started out
tonight with nonrefundable tickets to a honeymoon in
Texas."

"Why Texas?"

Tacked into the bulletin board above my desk was
the wedding-party guest list I had been mulling over.
Next to George's name was a question mark.

"All right," Alberta decided when I wouldn't
change the subject. "He left Bardstown more than an
hour ago. He called me from the Vogue. He said he
wanted to sit in the dark."

"He went to the movies?" The Vogue was a neighborhood theater that charged a dollar for revived
double features. It was one of George's favorite spots.
The last time we went out together we had seen *Alice's
Restaurant* and *Hair*.

"It's not too late to change your mind," Alberta

advised. She obviously knew the whole story, maybe more of it than I did. "I could explain to George."

W HERE ARE YOU GOING?" DAD ASKED at midnight when I came downstairs with my coat on. He was about to run the dishwasher.

"The Vogue."

"What starts at this hour?" He still worried about me.

"We'll see." I raised my eyebrows, smiled, and closed the door.

I drove to the theater without any plan beyond the point of intercepting George when he came out the exit. The night air was humid and breezy, heavy with the honeysuckle smell of late summer. The streets were deserted except for the night joggers, their backs and their shoes crisscrossed with strips of reflector tape. As my headlights caught them, one by one, they looked like floating, bouncing hyphens, disconnected and going nowhere. Nervously I punched the scan button on the radio and listened while the cursor crossed the band picking up and displaying three seconds of one station after another. "And the Lord sayeth to . . ." said a deep male voice, instantly replaced by "Baby, baby, baby, you're out of . . ." followed by ". . . tonight, with a forty percent possibility of . . ." and ". . . Milton. I never in a . . ."

There was a cassette in the slot and I pushed it in. Bonnie Raitt, naturally speaking to me alone, but by the time I got to the show my mood was better. Maybe George was my Nick of Time guy. Maybe this was all meant to be and we'd have a magic moment, a fitting match to his call. His face would shine when he saw me standing under a street lamp. We'd gallop toward each other in slow motion. He'd swing me around in the air and answer all my questions before I had to ask them.

The first thing I noticed was the marquee: *Help* and *A Hard Day's Night.* I found a parking place and turned off my headlights. There was the possibility that George had already departed, that he had called Alberta and tried to reach me at home or else left the state, but I didn't think so. Sometimes stories have to play themselves out.

At exactly twelve-eighteen a crowd of people emerged, stretching and talking, and George followed a beat later. He stopped, looked right and left, and then started walking in the opposite direction from where I watched. I opened my door, stood by the car.

"Need a ride?"

He stopped, turned his head, and squinted into

the darkness, betraying no indication that my voice was the sound in the world he had been most hoping to hear.

O NCE GEORGE WAS IN THE CAR, I considered where to go with him. We could hit the same Burger King he had called—forced symmetry— but it only stayed open until one and I didn't want to have to be interrupted. We could go back to my house, but that would mean getting Dad to bed before George and I could start to talk about real things. We could simply drive around, maybe out along River Road, but then I wouldn't be able to watch George's eyes. Whatever we had to say to each other, this was not a conversation I wanted to conduct in profile, and also I wanted my hands free, just in case. So I took us to the water company reservoir, off Frankfort Avenue. It was a dramatic setting at night, a rectangular man-made hill stuck like a mesa in the middle of the city. All the quiet machinery was housed in a turreted building constructed to look like a castle.

George followed me up the three flights of concrete stairs to the sidewalk that framed the main purification pool. We leaned on the wrought-iron fence and stared at the damp air. I was determined not to be the first one to speak.

The sky was the flat, blank silver of a lampshade illuminated by a dim bulb, a reflection of the city's lights off a ceiling of thick, low clouds. Little waves in the water caught the same dull shade, as did George's eyes when he finally turned toward me.

"Do you believe in telepathy?"

"I never thought that much about it." His question had to have a point. "Do you?"

"Two days ago I would have said no." George's tone was flat, as though he were making a public service announcement or informing his listeners that what they were about to hear was just a test of the Emergency Broadcast Network.

"But?"

"Bear with me, okay? The morning after I got your postcard?"

"Why didn't you call?"

George gave me a don't-rush-me look.

"Sorry."

"I go out to the kitchen and I think of how Mom always made me breakfast, even after her car wreck when she was limping."

George ran his fingers through his hair. Here it came, the telepathy part.

"You remember? When she went out for ice cream and slid off the shoulder in the rain?"

Alberta had told me the story more than once, always in a "Why me?" attitude for which there was no right response.

"Neapolitan," I reminded him. "That was the flavor of the ice cream."

"And suddenly I knew exactly how she felt when she went into that skid," George continued. He shook his head, as if he wanted to release the memory.

"I don't see . . ." I began.

"I mean I *really* knew how she felt, like I was inside her mind." George's voice suddenly went up a couple notches to where he was close to shouting. "No! No! No! No! Oh, shit! Help me! Oh, God!"

The loudness was shocking to hear. The words skipped over the water like flat rocks, and then just as quickly his pitch was back to normal.

"There wasn't anything I could do. I grabbed the table, I knocked off a glass."

I touched George's arm. It was stiff, braced against the fence as if warding off an impact.

"A bad dream," I offered by way of comfort.

"More than that," George insisted. "I knew things I couldn't have known. What it would feel like in the hospital. How sad I would be. How sad. How sad."

I thought he was going to cry. "Come on," I said. "Let's walk."

"You don't understand." George put his hands on my shoulders to focus my attention. "The same kind of thing happened all day yesterday. The newsbreak would come on the air and I'd feel inside myself every awful thing I heard. Hunger. Wars. Pollution. I couldn't shut it off."

"The feed?"

"Me, my brain. It was like I couldn't close my eyes. No matter what was in front of me, I always saw it in its worst moment. I was going crazy. Then I thought of you, getting married."

At last we were approaching where I wanted to go.

"You realized you loved me," I said helpfully and could have kicked myself. I didn't want to speak for George. I didn't know what I wanted him to say.

"You don't get it," he whispered, hoarse, emphatic. "I *knew* how you'd feel married. Bored. Desperate. I *knew*. I couldn't let you."

"Let me understand." I held on to George's arms just below the elbow. I could either lift him away from me or bring him closer. "You called to *save* me?"

"I *was* you," George yelled into my face. "I saw your future."

"You think a lot of yourself." I threw this off absently, evenly, because it was as though I had caught whatever power George was talking about and was looking at myself as I might turn out if I wasn't careful: stuck and wondering why. Married to an Alan or a George without ever actually choosing to do it. I saw

1 1 7

myself in Christmas greeting photographs, all the colors too bright and bleeding into one another. Settled, accounted for, filed away, defined by a stranger's vocabulary. I saw myself marching up in a line holding a numbered card, coming to a desk and dropping the card into a slot in the top of a box. Except that I hadn't done that. I had broken off my engagement, partly because Alan had been so careful to leave me precisely half the onion rings. I had jumped for *anything* instead of sticking with something sure. I was off the track, off the hook, and I found myself overcome with an emotion that I recognized the minute I stopped to name it: I was glad.

"It's not that," George was saying. "I don't know why it happened, but for one day I was more than myself. Or maybe my best self. I had empathy, complete, selfless love. And I couldn't keep still."

I nodded, too happy to speak. Louisville spread around below me in a great scattered circle of lights. I could smell mowed grass, hear a siren in the distance, puzzle out the black shape of my parked car.

George sighed, turned back to the fence. "The problem is," he said, "it switched off." He hung his head.

George and I didn't move. We were stuck in two separate pulls of where to go from here.

"Say it," urged George. His voice had a cringe to it.

"Be furious, tell me I screwed up your life. Push me in the water. Go ahead. Hit me. I have it coming."

I took a deep breath. There was a quality to the strange light, a combination of natural and artificial that made everything I saw stand out clearly, as if it were outlined by a Magic Marker. I could walk the tightrope of the fence. I could roll down the steep hill and never break a bone.

THE VASE

W HAT DISTINGUISHES THE VASE—
the first object I see when I use my key to enter the
dimness of my mother's kitchen from the light of a
warm Tuesday afternoon—is the fact that it's set out at
all. It's empty and beaded with moisture as if just
washed, of ordinary size, no more than a foot high and
six inches at the rim. The green glass is so dull and
thick that it siphons light. Off-center on the pure white
surface of the round table, its placement affronts this
house of organized closets and polished silver plate. It is

the sort of unintentional possession usually stored, once its florist's arrangement has withered, behind the closed doors of a lower cabinet, or packed, against the possibility of future need, in an attic box. And there for years forgotten.

Its purpose today, I instantly recognize, is declaration, the prelude to a story in which I will figure. Yellow mums or red carnations will spill again from its lip in my mother's memory, offered evidence to an occasion of my father's apology, floral encouragements proven false by the vast betrayal of his death. Before I escape through this room, I'll receive the whispered tale. My mother will touch the vase's contour, absently stroke its murky surface, then adjust its position to the exact bull's-eye of the tabletop as she speaks. She'll say it's mine now, not to neglect to take it when I go.

It will do me no good to protest, to plead with my mother to keep her own memento. I've tried that tack before, and have been contradicted by the sweep of her arm indicating the accumulated treasure that comes to me through her constantly revised will. "Let me enjoy the giving," she demanded last week in reference to a blanket reeking of camphor. But I shook my head, protested that I lacked room for it, and watched the disappointment line her face. In punishment, she stuffed the blanket into the trash, refused to let me change my mind.

In the past year we have played out many variations on this scene, from expressions of gratitude to hurtful indifference, and still, doled with each weekly visit, the unwanted inheritances continue. They have no consistent category, no pattern. My father's gold and onyx cuff links were succeeded by a vinyl tablecloth still sealed in plastic, and that in turn by chipped china plates, a photograph album whose only recognizable pictures were of my great-aunts in their youth, a fountain pen, and a floor lamp. And the blanket. My mother is determined to transfer herself to me one item at a time, to bind us through a bridge of things. When her house has been emptied into mine, there will be no choice but for her to follow, or for her to die.

T HOUGHT MOVES IN THE MIND faster and more fully than it can be expressed. It rolls like a tide littering a beach with scattered debris, then yields in the expanse of a pupil, in the refocus of vision, to accommodate the gloom of a forty-watt overhead bulb. The kitchen is empty, the countertops clean, the sink clear, the linoleum floor ivory with wax. Two framed rectangles of glass, one large, one smaller, have been propped against the washing machine, ready to replace screens in the storm door. From the living room I hear the sounds of music and applause, and the rhythmic creak of the rocking chair straining beneath my mother's weight.

I open the refrigerator and deposit the cheese, eggs, and bread she has requested. The shelves gleam a cold gray. They are stocked with the provisions of a woman who abhors waste and excess, the sustenance of a nun, of a prisoner: a half-full jar of instant coffee, a tinfoil-wrapped can of salmon, a tub of no-cholesterol margarine, its clear cover spotless. And on the bottom tray, for me, a thawing peach pie. I straighten my back, close the door. The applause becomes louder as I approach, louder, until I realize that my mother has joined the "Wheel of Fortune" studio audience and claps her own hands in approval of a spin I can't see.

She stills her chair when she becomes aware of me. Her shoulders bunch beneath her sweater and her green eyes dart to the TV screen as if to see how much of her private life I have caught. She sits with a half-gone box of dried apricots on her lap and a blue velvet couch pillow braced behind her back. Her feet are bare, the knuckles of her toes knotted from years of standing in laced nurse's shoes. Her white hair, stiff from the beauty parlor, the complicated curls interlocked tight as those on a marble statue, floats all but disconnected above the pale dome of her scalp. The effect is an illusion, a mask to her growing baldness, and she sees me notice.

"How long have you been spying on me?" Her voice is raw, irritated from nonuse.

"Who's ahead?"

She turns back to the TV. "I'm waiting for 'Star Search.' A repeat." She nods without emotion and sees into the future. "That redhead's going to win the one hundred thousand. But she doesn't hold a candle to her challenger."

I won't let her off that easily. "Who were you clapping for just now?"

She tilts forward, uses the momentum to propel herself out of the chair. Still in a crouch, she moves to the set and punches it off, furious to be discovered in an attitude that does not demand sympathy.

"You're like *him*." She means my father, the only "him" besides me in her vocabulary. "Light on your feet."

I shift my weight. "I should have called first."

She tightens her mouth and pushes past me into the narrow hall, disappears into the bathroom. The walls are thin, so I hear the click of the lock and then the rush of water in the sink, which lasts until after the toilet has flushed. Her privacy.

All around me, the floor is crowded with furniture.

The house where she lived with my father long after my sister and I moved away to our wasted educations was much larger than this one, both in the size and in the number of its rooms. The brocade couch, the maroon upholstered chairs, the coffee table and sideboards are the same as ever, but it is as if the walls surrounding them have shrunk, condensing the space. In my imagination I measure and weigh each item, wondering when it will be bequeathed me, whether it will jam through my front door, where I can fit it, to whom it can be sold or donated.

Some pieces, my mother has informed me, are earmarked for Marjorie, my sister who visits from Texas once a year and uses these forays to make her selections. On the underside of each hand-painted Bavarian plate displayed on the hutch is a torn strip of tan masking tape with "M." printed in blue ink. By right of her gender, Marjorie lays claim to all jewelry, and it has not escaped me that those articles to which she now confesses sentimental attachment, and has therefore branded, constitute the only genuine antiques.

My gaze strays to the center of the picture gallery on top of the television console, to a brass-framed photograph—a portrait, it was called when made—of Jill and Paul III and me, taken . . . when? I count back, remembering the night we stood in line at Sears in obedience to my mother's birthday command. It was not long before the divorce, so that would put it six years ago.

I was dressed in popular style—a powder blue suit and a flowered shirt with a wide, pointed collar. I wore my hair longer than now, and my left hand, marked with the thick wedding band that matched Jill's, rested on my son's shoulder. After the session we had gone to the boys' department to buy him summer pajamas. We found a short-sleeved pair in a material printed with red and blue sailboats. Jill chose a size too big, her eyes challenging me to object.

In the portrait Jill does not look happy, despite her camera smile. Her expression is flat, apprehensive. Did she know as early as that night? Had she already met Victor through the accountant for whom she did taxes part-time every winter? I study her face, but she reveals nothing that I didn't know at the time.

Paul, beneath my hand, is easier to read. He was then at an age when he still permitted Jill to dress him, yet he was old enough to look shamed by the coordinated match of his blue-and-white-striped T-shirt and pants. Jill held his hand to prevent him from biting his nails, though eventually we surrendered our campaign against this habit. When he was with me last month, he glared at my initial, automatic correction, and made no move to remove the tip of his finger from between his teeth. At thirteen, suffering through a two-week, boring visit, he was beyond any approach. If I nagged, he would ask Jill and Victor to make an excuse and keep him in Ohio at Thanksgiving.

M Y MOTHER RETURNS, CARRYING in her hand something dark, the size and shape of a hockey puck. She waits for my inquiring look, then hands over the object for me to examine.

"I've turned the house upside down," she complains. "How it got into the vanity below the sink I'll never know."

"It" is a piece of china pierced with small wells. A single flower stem can be fitted into each hole in order to equitably distribute a bouquet within a vase. My mother takes the thing back from me and pushes it into my breast pocket, where it bulges and pulls taut the buttons of my shirt. I keep my mouth shut. She knows I have seen her kitchen table and dares me to argue.

"There's pie," she says, lest I miss the point.

I confirm that there is.

"Peach." She wants more reaction, even enthusiasm, though the instant I show an interest she will begin to criticize the pastry, how it is never as good once frozen, how the fluted crust is too thick because she needs new glasses that she can't afford and wouldn't dream to ask me to buy, how she can only eat a small bite because her stomach wouldn't tolerate sweets, though she is cursed to crave them.

"Marjorie's favorite," I note, and skirt her quick glance. I walk to the TV and pick up my family picture. "Did you hear from Paul since he went back?"

"What do you expect?" she asks the wall. "I told him to write when he had news. But at least Jill called to say he arrived safe."

She pauses, and I am tempted to satisfy her, tempted to rail at her continued treasonous friendship with Jill. I have evidence that they frequently discuss me, and not favorably. Once when I called to speak to Paul, Jill answered the phone.

"A mustache," she laughed. "What next? Did it come out brown or gray?"

She could have had no other way of knowing than through my mother, who also disapproved. The next day I shaved my face clean.

"She and Victor are going on a trip to New York City," my mother announces. "Business."

She emphasizes the last word. I am the manager of a record store specializing in classical music, a not bad one, but Victor is an aerospace engineer, a step up for Jill, a man in national demand.

After the divorce, when I told my mother I was offended by her alliance with my ex-wife, she answered with eyes cast to the ceiling and an exasperated sigh. *"She* is the mother of my grandchild. Just because *you* couldn't keep her happy is no reason to sever my ties."

But it's more than that. If there were no Paul, my mother would still maintain the link. She prizes her bonds to long-distance women, to Marjorie and Jill. The record of her telephone calls to them gives her a topic.

"Can you imagine?" she asked last month, showing me the bill. "Twenty-one minutes to Houston? Fourteen to Dayton? What could we have found to pass all that time?"

WELL," I SAY. "I CAN'T STAY. I ONLY came by to drop off your necessities and see how you were."

"How was I?" My mother holds out her heavy arms in straight lines and revolves a full circle for my inspection. She has washed her face. When she pauses, her head tilted back, she exaggerates the difference in our heights.

"The same as ever," I observe.

"Ha!" Her look shouts that there is much she could tell but doesn't because I am too slow to understand. "That's what *he* used to say." She moves toward the kitchen.

129

"He was right."

My mother's back freezes, recording this challenge. My words goad her to a new level of alertness, and she turns, narrowing her eyes.

"What's *that* supposed to mean, I wonder?"

"It isn't supposed to mean anything. But you don't change. It's one of the things about you. He probably noticed it too."

A flush spreads from a place below my mother's left ear to color her cheek and neck. She wets her lips with her tongue, prolonging her outrage.

"He wouldn't notice a train if it crushed him." As always, she refers to my father as if he has not been gone nine years. "You don't call this *changed?* Living hand to mouth in this cramped box? Having nothing to look forward to but you waltzing in and saying 'I can't stay'? Losing my hair? Having to please and thank-you every move you make?" She punctuates her words by slapping the doorjamb with the flat of her hand.

I am stung by her sarcastic mimicry, by the sour whine she has thrown into her voice when she repeats my words, and that leaves me speechless. She takes this as a sign of weakness.

"You think you're some kind of a prince. Don't give me that hangdog face. Don't expect me to apologize. You always did and always will."

She blocks the door like a closed gate. I take two

deep breaths, let the oxygen sink into my diaphragm while I remind myself of her age, of the trouble it would be to make things right if I let myself become emotional, of how, through guilt or uncaged anger, she would eventually reduce me to apology. I fight for control and gain it.

"If you want company, I'll stay."

"Stay, go, I don't care. What good are you?" She does not respect the calm in my voice.

"What good? I'm here. I do your shopping. I check—"

"You're here but you're not here. Don't make me your excuse."

I restrain myself from echoing her accusation. She can pick at my patience worse than anyone.

"You don't believe that. Why would you say such a thing?" I make my voice light, but in spite of myself I am angry now, hurt to be so misinterpreted.

Our eyes meet for the first time. Then she loses energy, or interest, and rubs her hands as if to dry them against the material of her dress where it shapes her hips. A hush blows through the room like forced air from a furnace, fixing a memory of our exchange that I will carry home and consider.

For an instant, it all evaporates: the clothes we wear in order to be invisible, the words we speak without meaning or hearing, the outlines into which we allow ourselves to be fitted. For an instant, the blur focuses. I don't like this woman, cannot contact a feeling of affection for her. And I know, without the comfort of doubt or dispute, that to her I am a stranger she has lost the will to love.

"Pay no attention to me." She breaks the mood at last. "I'm alone too much and you're too easy to take on."

"Mom." I smile, relax my neck, and realize that I still hold the photograph from her television. I return it to its place and search for a safe subject.

"Paul will be okay," I say, inviting her agreement. "He's quite the young man."

"They want me to come visit, as his grandmother."

"You should go." I'm proud of my generosity.

She regards me with an attitude halfway between fatigue and fury, and speaks in a new, neutral tone. "*You* should go. No, I don't mean to Jill's, I mean now. Go on. You were in a hurry."

When she's like this, I don't want to leave. "Not before I have a cut of that pie," I say. "Since you defrosted it."

"The crust is cardboard." She disappears into the kitchen and I hear the refrigerator swing open, hear the clash of silverware in a drawer.

"I don't hear me complaining." Behind the television the front door is permanently closed with two locks and a chain, even in August. My mother fears theft as though she has something here to steal.

"What are you so worried about?" I call.

She comes to the doorway, a fork and knife in each hand.

The heavy ceramic base in my pocket drags my shirt so low on the left side that I feel it lump above my ribs with every breath. I silently count to four, then draw it out, offer it to make peace.

"I will die in this house," my mother states, staring past me. "Won't be found for a week's time."

There is no answer to her words. I let them alone. "I thought you could put it with the vase so I wouldn't forget."

She shakes her head and walks back to the table. Let her tell Marjorie. Let her confide in Jill, who will surely have old injuries of her own to exhume. I am who I am.

I follow into the kitchen and take the chair that's pulled out. There is a plate set before me, and on it is a small, perfect wedge of pie. My mother's filling never runs, she is known for that. Her secret is an extra measure of tapioca.

My mother ignores me, continues to rummage

among her utensils in a counter drawer, searching for something. At last she turns, a twist of satisfaction to her mouth, and drops a fistful of matched iced-tea spoons into the vase. They make a harsh noise as they fall. They are like sticks down a well, too short to rise above the rim.

ME AND
THE GIRLS

FOR FUGITIVE, EASY PART IS 2 ELEPHANTS

For four years, Arlan Seidon and two female
elephants, Tory and Duchess, have been fugitives from
the New Jersey police. "I realize this looks like a
story about an old kook who took two elephants
and ran away," Mr. Seidon said in a rare phone
interview from some place; he wouldn't say where.
"But I couldn't let my girls be abused. Sorry, I
always refer to them as my girls. They're like family."

MICHAEL WINERIP, *The New York Times*

ME AND THE GIRLS ARE FINE
now, considering.

Duchess got her ear caught in the sliding door of an
eighteen-wheeler. She didn't escape in time, but who
knew the thing was going to start? When we snuck in
after midnight to escape the steady downpour—we

reached the rest stop overland, from behind—I figured the snoring driver was out till dawn, sure. But four A.M. I heard this electronic-sounding beeping, from his wristwatch I now realize.

At the time, I forget what I thought. I was in dreamland. Me and the girls were by a lake in Africa or somewhere, throwing water on ourselves. All the god-damn water you could wish for. Hosing each other down, all cool and clean, not like these lousy backyard swimming pools we've had to use lately. They're full of poisonous chlorine and I hate for the girls to get that stuff up their snoots, but I ask you, what choice is there?

Anyway, once I put two and two together and opened my eyes, I felt the rumble of the diesel turning over, and in the gray light all I could see was the girls' eyes, kind of yellow and watching me for what to do. They've come to respect me. I was sacked out next to Tory that night—I try to spread it around, take turns, you know—and I automatically reached over and scratched her wrinkled forehead. Poor old thing, the bristles of her hair were stiff as wire. She snorted and began that rocking motion she has to do before she can reach a standing position.

Duchess got the idea a minute later, by which time I heard the truck go into first gear. The taillights switched on, turning the asphalt red behind the back set of tires. I hopped into its rosy glow and tapped with my stick to signal the girls to follow. Big as she is, Tory is a dainty one, light on her feet for her weight, and the ground barely shook as she hauled herself out. Duchess, though, she's not at her best in the mornings even under prime conditions. First she opened her yap and let loose with a long complaint about being wakened up so early, then she takes it into her pea brain to back herself off, a leg at a time, as though she were inching into one of those swimming pools from the shallow end. I can tell you, what remained of the full moon went into total eclipse as her behind blocked half the sky. I urged her to get the lead out, but being Duchess she wouldn't rush.

I felt halfway grateful to the driver who'd provided our shelter—not that he'd issued any formal invitations—and just a touch guilty about the presents Tory had left him. When nature calls, she answers, no matter where she is. All she needs is a clear spot about three feet square. It's her way of saying "I've been here." I attribute her brass to the fact that she got a lot of laughs and applause for this practice when she was young, just starting her show business career.

Anyhow, I slammed shut that road jockey's back panel before he spewed toxic waste or whatever the hell he was trucking down the Garden State Parkway. I'll allow I was overanxious, but everything happened so quick. The tires spun, and Duchess gave a scream because when I slammed the door I locked the tip of her ear inside the truck. It was some contest, I tell you, Duchess tugging one way, the Mack pulling the other. It was a scene in suspended animation, nobody going nowhere, exhaust fumes and the smell of burning rubber rising like swamp gas, like something out of one of those crapshoot Japanese monster movies, *Mothra vs. Rodan,* both sides equally matched. I can't speculate on what the other truckers thought when they rubbed the sleep out of their eyes at the noise and drank it all in. I know one of them honked his horn, as if an ordinary sound would make the horrible vision disappear.

Well, no battle lasts forever, and in the end the machine proved the stronger, though not by much. When the break finally came, the truck had stored so much spare energy that it popped from that parking space like it had grown turbo drive, like a pilot sprung from an ejector seat, and the tip of Duchess's ear went along for the ride. As the vehicle shot toward the ramp, barreling through line after white line of headlamps that had been switched on in the ruckus, I caught a glimpse of the driver's face reflected in his left rearview. He was fighting for control of the wheel, all the while trying to see behind him what the holdup had been. When his look connected with Duchess's, mad as she was and ready for round two, he floored the gas pedal and took his chances with slick roads.

I confess, there was a part of me that envied his flight. I could see it: in an hour or so he'd slow down, pull into a café, and order up a fried breakfast. While it cooked he'd tell his tale to anybody who'd listen. His eyes would be wild, full of the wonder of encountering one of the monsters of the road, an instant truckstop legend. After a day's travel and a full night's sleep he'd begin to doubt his own memory, to throw in a laugh or two when he repeated the events. In his tale, Duchess would grow horns, shark teeth, a lion's mane. She'd chase him for ten miles instead of holding her ground like she did, her big square feet braced in the soft dirt. Sooner or later that driver would finish his run and go home to his wife and kids, and the adventure would turn into nothing more than a bedtime story with a happy ending: the hero escaped.

Which is an option not available to yours truly. That's what happens when you take responsibility in your own hands, when you step out of the crowd and fight for justice, when your beliefs run away with you. I never could tolerate mistreatment of creatures dumber than me. That late-summer day six weeks ago I wasn't figuring on becoming a fugitive from blind justice, but when I passed Duchess and Tory—I knew their names from the program—all caged up and sad-eyed, smelling like a stink factory and expected to sleep in damp straw, my heart went out to them. Earlier I had witnessed their act in the center ring, but now they didn't look like circus stars. I walked closer, held out the remains of my hot-dog sandwich the same as you would to a pitiful stray on the street, and damn if that Tory didn't reach out for it, gentle as a lamb, and wrap it into her hooter. It was the trust that got to me. She didn't know who I was from spit—that hot-dog sandwich could have been poisoned, filled with glass splinters—but she took a chance on me, recognized something in my face that most people always miss.

I hung around till long after dark, till after the crowds cleared out and the crew hit the sack. I waited till almost dawn, then I sneaked up close and pulled the heavy pin from the lock. At the sound, both girls startled out of their socks.

"Shh," I said. "It's a friend."

I swear to you they understood my language. They fairly tiptoed, for them, down the platform stool I set before their door and followed me, one behind the other, through the deserted parking lot. Like I say, pure trust. All that night we kept off beaten paths, made our way across open fields, then slept through the daylight hours under the cover of a wrecked barn.

Our getaway made the newspapers, of course. I

plucked one from a doorstep after our second night on the run and there they were, big as life, their picture on the front page. What's more, the public interviewed by the reporter had all manner of opinions and theories to explain the mysterious disappearance: aliens, the owners of a rival carnival, an attention-grabbing stunt. Not a soul guessed the thirst for freedom, that's how sour this world has become.

It won't be easy getting the girls back where they belong, where they can roam, take up with others of their own kind, raise a family as nature intended. I don't claim to have a plan, but something will occur to me—I depend on inspiration. Until that time we're heading south, slow and sure as glaciers, following the riverbeds, just us three.

JEOPARDY

THE BACKSEAT AND FLOOR OF my blue '89 Buick LeSabre are awash in industry pamphlets and reprints, the mess a result of my stopping too quickly at too many red lights. Next to me on the passenger side slumps a trash bag full of empty Hardee's and Burger King wrappings, their contents consumed on the fly. I have this idea to recycle—inspired by a panicky talk show I tuned in on the long drive from Billings to Bozeman—but all that happens is greater accumulation. That's the sum of good intentions.

On this Friday morning at the end of a long week my schedule puts me into Kalispell, a spic-and-span town at the northwest tip of Nowhere, Montana, beautiful to look at but cold, and I don't mean only climate-cold, either. All the docs are clustered in two or three professional buildings, cement-block forts with Muzak and back issues of *People* in waiting rooms guarded by blond, Charlie's Angels–haired women. I check my list: my first stop is Dee Dee, about whom I have noted in the margin: "Kid with allergy. Likes Dairy Queen blizzard (tropical?). 6."

The "6" refers to the minutes of chitchat it usually takes to admit me to the inner sanctum. I get paid by the number of scrips—physician signatures acknowledging our conversations—that I collect, not by time spent or volume of orders. It all boils down to human contact, though the verbal conversation is pretty much one way, me to her, with her replies made in eyebrows, sighs, shrugs, and head movements.

"Lots of pollen around, huh? Hey, maybe your little boy . . . That's not him in the frame on your desk? I can't believe how he's grown. No. . . . Maybe he could try this new inhaler. It's a miracle worker. Just remember, you don't know where you got it, right, because I could get in major trouble and it's just because we're friends, you know, and I had allergies myself as a kid. Sure I do. Three puffs a day this time of year, and not a wheeze. Don't mention it, I just hope it helps him, because that's what counts, that's why I'm in this business, to help people. And if you could just get me in to see the physician for five minutes, max, I want to tell him about this product, not yet commercially available—amazing stuff, really, the cutting edge. I'm positive he'd want to know about it direct, not hear it from his competition or from a patient who had read about it in *Time* or somewhere. Well, not yet, but they've assigned a science reporter. I'll just sit over here and straighten out my schedule—I've got more appointments than I can handle and I just wish all of them were . . . No, whenever, no problem, no hurry. Forget I'm here, but if he has three minutes, I'll be quick. Cross my heart. So . . . hey, are you still using that old pen from my last visit? That's kind of sentimental. I'm touched. But let me give you a new one. Take one for your son too. Good, two. Kids lose things. Tell me about it."

I check my watch. Six minutes flat.

And then I sit, not watching Dee Dee not watch me, and read an article about John Travolta's happy marriage. Every once in a while I make a point of catching Dee Dee's eye, and salute. Meanwhile she waves in a procession of strep throats and backaches, varicose veins and odd pains in the chest. I make a game of guessing the ailment as well as the amount of consult time by focusing on the mouths: indignant-grim versus scared-grim, ready-to-be-mad versus ready-to-cry. I'm the only cheerful presence—besides Dee Dee's hair—in the room, the only healthy delegate in a convention of germs. Still, inside an hour, I'm out the front door with three signatures.

Next on the list comes Lisa, the mother type. She presides over a whole clinic of potential scrip-signers, all stacked neatly behind a single swinging half-door. Ducks in a row, fish in a barrel. Those docs are so overworked with Medicaids that they're glad for the diversion, actually ask questions about the product to keep me talking. They see my face and head for Mr. Coffee like kids who'd rather play at cleaning their rooms than do their homework, or people so bored that they sit around their houses waiting for Jehovah's Witnesses to drop by. The answer to a rep's prayer. With them it isn't getting your toe in the door, it's escaping before dark, not a dilemma I often encounter and not one I'm complaining about either.

Sympathy's the key to Lisa's lock, as it is with a lot of them. You open your heart wide enough, she presses the buzzer under her desk and it's Hello Sesame. The challenge is keeping the story straight. What sad tale did I use last time? Which detail made her pupils tighten, her neck muscles tense to attention? With the pity freaks my life has to be soap opera, and believe me, these women have a memory. Lisa almost trips me up halfway through today's installment of My Unfair Divorce.

"I thought you said you'd been happily married for four years before you got the boot," she challenges, her face balled up into a loose fist. "Now, suddenly, it's three."

Call her Perry Mason.

"Well, it's both, I guess." I'm thinking fast. "See, I don't like to admit it but we lived together for a year before we actually tied the knot." This is a calculation on my part, a hope that Lisa, the romantic, will forgive shacking up more than she will gross exaggeration.

She shakes her head in a disapproval that's more interested than serious. "They do that now."

I nod, sharing her despair at the decline of morals. *"Her* idea," I confess, seizing sudden inspiration and running with it. "I'm the old-fashioned type."

I hold up my left hand to show I still wear a ring, even separated. I let that band of gold speak volumes about the kind of guy I am.

Lisa's eyes approve, though I notice that her ring finger's bare. In unrequited love with one of the docs is my bet, one of those men whose wives don't understand the pressures of the medical profession, Lisa's specialty.

"What did you say her name was?"

Great. A test. I flip through my mental Rolodex. Betsy? Maria? Luanne? How did I read Lisa the first time? Not ethnic, certainly, so Maria's out, but am I married up or down? Am I left for a rich boy or for a bum?

"Betsy?" I venture. Betsy the bitch whose father had opposed our marriage because I wasn't good enough for her. Betsy, who even now, while I'm out trying to make an honest dollar, is probably sipping a gin and tonic at the country club with the pro after her tennis lesson.

"That's right," Lisa recalls. Bingo. "Well, you hang in there, honey. One of these days you're going to meet a girl who'll appreciate you. I promise."

Right, I think, and then what? How many visits of happily ever after before you get bored? No way. So I sigh, sorry for myself but brave, uncomplaining.

"I'm staying with my dad now," I add for good measure. You can't beat the truth for authentic details. "He's been kind of low since he was laid off his job. Watches 'Jeopardy' three times a day on the satellite dish, even tapes it."

Lisa nods. I'm a good son, too. There's no end to my virtue.

"I know they're looking forward to seeing you." She gestures toward the examining rooms with her chin, trying to cheer me up. "It won't be long. I'll arrange it so they're all free at the same time. Why should *you* have to wait?"

T H E   E N D   O F   T H E   D A Y   I   R E S E R V E for Patt. She's not bad-looking in a kind of white starched way. I could imagine her taking off her glasses, shaking out her hair, unlacing her shoes. We have this flirt thing going, the game being that I'm chasing and she's holding me at bay, just barely. One of these days, if I don't watch out, she'll decide to take me up on dinner, whatever.

"So, is the divorce final?" she wants to know first thing, giving me a wink. "No more Maria?" Her fingers caress the sample box of lavender bath beads, the exact size and shape of Som-U-Rest, the sleeping pill I represent on the side.

"Maria who?" With Patt I sort of sit on the edge of her desk, my thigh brushing the telephone so she has to consciously avoid touching me if a call comes in.

"Then why still the ring? You carrying a torch?"

I look at my finger. Damn. "Can I be honest?"

That snags her. It's almost too easy.

"See, in my profession I meet a lot of women, some of them lonely."

Patt could imagine.

"Well, you understand, a man on the road. Some

might think I'm looking for a one-night stand, which I'm not, but all those jokes about traveling salesmen? It's a, you know, occupational stereotype."

Patt snorts, warning me I am pushing this maybe too far.

"I can read your mind," I inform her. "You think because I kid around with you I do it with everybody, right? That I come on to all the women I meet?"

"Well . . . ?" Patt sees the trap, but plows ahead anyway.

I close my eyes, open them, then speak slowly, as though revealing something that isn't easy to admit. "Truth, okay? The ring's protection. It says, 'Sorry, taken,' which avoids misunderstanding. Hey, listen to me. Now you'll think I spill my life story to everybody. It isn't even that interesting."

"No," Patt automatically objects. "No, it is, really."

"Don't be nice, all right? It's just with you I feel I can be . . . what? Myself?"

She doesn't move, expecting me to go on. Instead I let the silence grow, wait her out. Finally she reaches over, touches my hand where it rests on my leg.

"I told you, don't be nice."

"I'm not being nice," Patt says. "I hear you, is all."

A woman and her little boy come through the door from the examining rooms. Patt and I both sit up straighter, as though caught in the act.

"He says to squeeze us in next Tuesday," the woman tells Patt, who searches the book for a free fifteen minutes.

"Tuesday he's solid."

"He *said*," the woman insists.

"I'll have to do some shuffling." Patt's not a bit pleased with the physician's disregard for her careful appointment keeping. She looks up at me, Mr. Reasonable, not asking for a thing of her that's hard. "Why don't you run in while I make a couple of calls," she suggests, and glances at the clock. "Maybe we can continue this conversation later. If you're free."

I give her a look like, are you kidding?

Of course by the time I come out, my samples bag a little lighter, Patt has remembered an engagement she can't get out of. I grab my shirt, try to hold my breaking heart in one piece, but the fact is I'm relieved at the prospect of a quiet night at the Outlaw Inn, writing up my report, filing my receipts. After a day of smiling, being whoever people need me to be, I'm ready to grab a bite, call Dad, do some work, then crash in front of the in-room HBO.

THE OUTLAW IS BIG, TWO INDOOR pools big, with an instant-cash machine in the lobby, the accommodations of choice for Salt Lake City–based

Delta crews on a layover and for businessmen like my-self, even though it does come on a bit strong. Each building has a theme—the roundup, Indians, bank rob-beries, what have you—that leaks from the halls into the individual guest rooms, and the restaurant menu features "a taste of Montana," which means huckle-berries dumped into everything from breast of chicken to Irish coffee.

First thing after check-in, I try Dad to see how he's making out. He and I have become one of those can't live with him/can't live without him relationships after batching it together for a year. I let the phone go five rings before I bag it and head for the lounge. Probably he stayed late at the library, boning up for the next "Jeopardy" open-call contestants' competition. I figure a couple or three B & B's have my name on them after the day I've put in.

The Branding Iron is Friday-full. I stand in the en-trance and let my eyes adjust to the smoky light while I check for a familiar face. You do this job long enough and you meet people, on the road like yourself. Sure enough, sitting alone in a booth there's Jim Dohene, a rep for a medical supplies concern out of Denver.

As I head across the room, I inventory what facts I've stored about his life: married, no kids; about thirty-five thousand dollars a year; drives an Olds; not too bad in the sack.

The last time I saw him was Spokane a year ago. We both had a few drinks and started trading war stories, tales only a fellow rep would understand the full significance of, and over the course of an hour or two, each of us taking turns standing another round, we built what I can only call a sense of trust between us. Then, one thing led to another, as it sometimes will do.

On the road, trust makes or breaks you. You have to know the odds when you hear a lead about a doc or a secretary, because it can backfire in a major way. Somebody might say: "Take the aggressive tack with that one. She folds like an accordion." Or, "Be sure to call him by his first name. He hates that formal crap." If the advice is accurate, it's time-saving, important to know. It could be three, four personal visits before you psyched it out for yourself. But if it's a curve ball, if she says, "Fuck you, buddy" when you get pushy, or he goes, "I spent eight years and a hundred thousand bucks to be addressed as *doctor* except by my closest friends," it's damage that can't easily be repaired.

Jim, I recall as I squeeze his shoulder, waking him up from wherever his mind has wandered, is okay. He clued me that Kathi in Missoula was a sucker for chocolate, and my next swing through Montana I scored three scrips in thirty minutes.

"What's happening, stranger?" I say in greeting.

"Still raking it in with that new line of double-carbon prescription forms?"

"God, the word gets out." Jim pats my hand, good sign number one. "Such as you left a trail of artificially mellow desk clerks in Great Falls last time you passed through. What do you use, a stun gun?"

"That isn't what she called it this afternoon." I make a face, thinking of Patt. "But what can I say? Some products sell themselves." I drop into the seat opposite and blow a kiss to the waitress to get her attention.

"I guess that's why you're here alone."

"Doesn't mean I have to leave that way." I raise my shoulders, hold up my palms, and provide him an easy out if he wants it. "And anyway, they never stay the night. I guess the husband would catch on."

"In your dreams. What's that new pill you're dealing got in it, anyway?"

We small talk like that back and forth, ironing out the kinks, giving us each time. Jim gets to the tape before me.

"So," he asks, pairing up two significant facts of my life at the same moment. "You still unattached, and how's your dad doing?"

I give him credit. No wonder he pulls in the bucks.

"Sorry to say, and okay, considering," I answer.

Jim shakes his head, understanding.

"I just tried to call him, but no answer," I continue, deciding to tackle the second point first. This early in the evening there's no need to rush if we both want to go there. "Probably out on the town."

"Party animal." Jim nods, raises his margarita. "Must run in the family."

Number two. I take his meaning, clink glasses. "So, been through Spokane lately?"

Jim pauses his drink in midair, cocks his head as if searching his memory banks, then puts his glass to his lips and takes a deep swallow.

"Spokane, Spokane, Spokane?" He gives his I've-just-made-a-sale smile. "I can't remember the last good night's sleep I had in that town."

"You can't, huh?"

"Let's see. Wait a minute, wait a minute, it's coming back to me, kind of in a hangover haze. The Sheraton, right?"

Beneath the table our knees bump. I signal the waitress. "Mine," I tell Jim. "I've got some catch-up to play."

He settles back into his seat. Now that we both know where we're headed, we can relax.

"So, your dad . . ."

"I'm not going to kid you. He's obsessed. I tried to get him on Prozac, but no. He'd rather follow his dream to land a spot on a quiz program, to show the world how smart he is."

"He needs to get out, meet people," Jim says. "Have some fun."

"Life's too short not to," I agree, and lay a ten down on the table to wait for our drinks. "You grab the opportunity when it presents itself or it passes you standing still."

Jim nods. He buys that theory one hundred percent and is ready and able to prove it.

"Which building they put you in?" I ask. "You a cowboy tonight?"

"Everybody's a cowboy in Montana after the sun goes down. It's a state of mind. You eat yet or what?"

I glance at my watch and see it's only eight-thirty. Too early to head upstairs, and we're both still way too sober anyhow. "Well, I had this hot date," I say. "But we must have got our signals crossed."

Jim pushes the menu in my direction. "I'd recommend the trout. It was fresh . . . once. So who did you see today?"

"I started with Dee Dee."

"Her kid's nose still a faucet?"

L ATER IN THE DARK, KEPT AWAKE by Jim's snores, I punch in Dad's number by touch, counting each of the little buttons and hoping I don't make a mistake and wake up a stranger in the middle of the night. I don't plan to talk when he answers, just hear his "Hello" to make sure he made it home all right, and then hang up. I let the damn thing ring a long time. Maybe he unplugged the phone, got absent-minded, and left it that way. Maybe he covered it with a pillow and is sleeping too soundly. Maybe he stashed it in the refrigerator again.

Dad lets the details slide. An idea man, he calls himself, always one step ahead, but in fact he usually has too many plans going at once.

"I should have been an architect," he informs me the night before I left. We're sitting on the couch, naturally watching his "Jeopardy," his steady beat since he was force-retired from the TV station.

"You don't have the patience," I tell him. The woman in the middle is beating the two-time champ. She's on a roll, marching down World Geography toward the $1,000 square. Alex Trebek smiles as she buzzes in again.

"I love that blueprint paper," Dad says. His eyes stay fixed on the screen, ready. "All you need is a ruler and the right kind of eraser. Supplies you can carry in your back pocket, stuff you can work with out of your own home."

The Daily Double is under the $600 and the woman goes for broke, her whole stash of $3,100. She's nervous and eager, like a person high above a pool on a springboard, thinking out a half-gainer. The answer box swings around: "Belgian Congo."

"What is Zaire?" Dad shouts.

The woman licks her upper lip, juggling countries. The other two contestants are rooting against her.

"You just have to learn the symbols," Dad continues on his other track. "Windows, closets. The doors are drawn half-open to show the direction of their swing. You can mock in the landscaping, everything. You're your own boss. All that matters is your imagination, and that gets better and better with experience."

"Zaire," the woman announces at last, pleased with her memory. When there's no applause from the studio audience she looks unsure. "It *is* Zaire," she insists hopelessly. Alex shakes his head. He's sorry.

"In Double Jeopardy the answer has to be in the form of a question," he reminds her. The woman's money screen blips. Wipeout.

"A pool is nothing," Dad says. "Four lines at right angles."

"Who's this house for, anyway?" I ask him.

"Not my grandchildren, that's for damn sure."

I tense up, ready to go another round, but this time

he only winks at me, nods toward the hallway. "Thirsty?"

"I could."

"Get me one too, while you're up." He's tricky.

I push myself out of my chair, go to the kitchen, open the refrigerator. Meanwhile I hear Dad switch channels to the station, Channel 7, that let him go. He does that from time to time, hoping to see snow, but when I come back into the living room empty-handed, everything on-screen appears normal, except there's no sound, thanks to the mute button. Ed Finley, about whom Dad has some strong negative emotions, is standing in front of a weather map pointing to a red lightning bolt in the vicinity of Ohio and working his mouth, talking and smiling, his little pig eyes as desperate as ever.

"We're all out of beer but the phone was in there."

"They could get a trained seal to do that." Dad points his thumb toward Ed. "Hold a stick in its mouth, clap with its flippers. Did I tell you how much take-home he gets?"

Ed Finley was not in Dad's corner when it counted, despite their long professional association on opposite sides of the #2 camera. Now, as I watch, the weatherman opens a large umbrella decorated with happy faces, meaning rain tomorrow.

"The telephone?" I ask.

Dad sighs, switches back to "Jeopardy," now in the last write-down question phase.

"It got on my nerves," Dad says, irritated. "I let it cool off."

The topic is the U.S. Presidency and the answer is Harry Truman's vice president. The three contestants screw up their faces, chew on their magic pencils, wait for inspiration. Finally, as the theme music winds down, they each scribble on the pads in front of them, but without conviction. You can tell the Zaire woman has done it again, bet over her head.

"Who is Alben W. Barkley?" Dad yells at the TV. "I win."

One after another the contestants come up with zero, except for the woman. She learned her lesson after all and has held back a dollar, and that gets her a ticket to tomorrow's show. The way she crows you'd think she's won the Publishers Clearing House sweepstakes instead of guessing Al Smith and losing $1,600.

I WAKE UP ALONE IN MY BED STILL wearing my half-buttoned shirt. The TV is on, sun is pouring through the space where the blinds don't quite meet, and a line of light shows under the bathroom door. I listen for the sound of the shower.

"You in there?" I call. No answer. The room feels

empty, though I have no recollection of Jim leaving. I have some difficulty even remembering what we got into last night.

I roll onto my stomach, reach for the phone, and dial Dad. The digital clock reads seven-twelve. After ten rings I give up and stare at the receiver as if it can tell me where the fuck he is. "I should call somebody." I must say this aloud, because I hear my own advice. I try to think of logical explanations: the lines are down, he's brushing his teeth, I forgot to use the correct area code. I dial his number again, listen to the ring while I get out of bed, dig my address book out of my case, and look up Dad's neighbor, Mrs. Kelsey.

"I'm overreacting," I explain when I tell her why I'm calling, "but if you could just check?"

"The newspaper was on his porch last night," she whispers, ominously proven right in her suspicions. "Still folded."

"I'll hang on," I tell her. "I'll wait while you go knock."

I T ' S A L M O S T T E N O ' C L O C K B Y T H E time I get done talking with the ambulance and the coroner and a funeral home whose name popped into my head. There's nothing left for me to do before I head back to Tacoma except report in to the district manager and have her cancel the rest of my appointments.

When I've finished all the business, I suddenly can't catch my breath. A panic rises in me, steady as water running into a tub, and I think I'm going to pass out. Somehow this is a familiar feeling—asthma, my chest squeezing shut. It comes back to me: I'd wake up like this and Dad would appear next to my bed with a brown grocery bag. He'd bunch it around a small opening and make me breathe into it while he counted. One, two, three, four, four and a half, five. By the time I got to ten I was back in control.

I look around the room and all I can find is a plastic laundry sack in a bureau drawer. It will have to do. I gather the opening into a tunnel, blow inside until my lungs are empty, hold them that way, then draw in slowly. Again. I see the sides of the bag move, expand and contract with the force of my oxygen. I don't know how many times I do this, but when I stop I don't need the bag anymore, and I have an idea.

I ask the motel operator for Jim's room.

"I'm sorry, sir. Mr. Dohene checked out a little over two hours ago."

I imagine Jim all brushed and neat. He's nobody I think of from one month to the next, so why can't I let it go? If we run into each other again and we're both free and in the mood, fine. If not, no biggie. Still, I call his company in Denver, pretend I'm a relative who needs to know his schedule.

"Is this a medical emergency or a personal matter?" the receptionist inquires, following procedure before releasing information. She might have to explain her reasons to Jim or to her boss and is covering her ass.

"A death," I say. For some reason I use my salesman's voice, the one that gets me through the door to the inner offices, the one they can't resist.

"Just one moment, please."

She smells a practical joke or worse, another rep trying to beat her guy to an appointment. She'll bump the call up the line to someone used to saying "no." I can tell the truth, some part of it. Jim and I are old friends who had dinner, a few drinks. Fast-forward through the part about wearing each other out all night and get to the punch line: I just heard that my dad passed away six hundred miles from here and I don't want to be alone, okay?

While I wait, listening to the piped music playing over the receiver in between recorded commercials for the company's products, mentally rehearsing my story, I glance around the room. Towels everywhere, my shorts still where Jim tossed them behind the chair, the ice bucket full of water, my sample case open on the floor.

"Screw it," I say into the phone. If I need comfort, I'll prescribe it for myself. I reach for my appointment book and dial Patt's office before I remember that today's Saturday. What's her last name? Higgins? No, that's Lisa. Jones, Smith, Robinson. Peters! Double T double P is how I've stored it in my memory. I locate the Kalispell directory and scroll down the possibilities. No Patt or P, but wait, there is: Bob and Patt, on Seventh Street South. Bob?

I recognize her voice right off when she finally answers.

"Guess who?" I say. "Just wondering if your previous engagement is out of the way."

There's a long pause and for a minute I think she doesn't place me. "It's Don," I remind her. "From yesterday."

"Hi, *Sally*," Patt answers, bearing down on the name. "Hey, I can't talk now. Bob and I are in the middle of something, if you know what I mean."

"How about later? Just to, you know, talk?"

"Mmmm. That's too bad. Can I call you back, like on *Monday* or something?"

"I'm only in town today, but I could wait around for you."

"Great. Talk to you after the weekend."

"You don't even know where I'm staying. I'm—"

"Sally, I've really got to run. Say hello to Rick."

Dial tone. Okay. I turn to Higgins, and there she is, Lisa. No disguise. I imagine her reaction to my news, all sympathy and concern. She'll want me to come to dinner, probably, and maybe I'll take her up on it. I don't have to be in Tacoma until tomorrow.

"Lisa, it's Don Banta." I identify myself right off.

"Who?"

"Don. We talked at your office? I used to be married to Betsy?" I'm proud of myself for recalling this detail with no prompting.

"Who?"

"I'm a drug rep."

"Oh. Right, right. The one who lives with his father. I'm sorry. At the end of the week I leave the office at the office. What can I do for you?"

"Well, I was hoping you were free. For lunch? There's something I want your advice about."

"My advice?"

"I don't want to go into it over the phone."

"That sounds mysterious, but it won't work out for today. I'm running my kids to ten things at once: piano, gymnastics, skating, a birthday party."

Kids. "I assumed you were single."

"Only in my prayers. But really, if you want to tell me what you need, maybe there's something—*Teresa, give that to her!* This place is a zoo."

"No, that's great. You're busy. I'll catch you the next time through."

"Okay, if you're sure. Bye-bye."

THAT LEAVES ONLY DEE DEE, AND her line's busy. While I wait to try again I can't keep my mind off Dad. He drives me nuts. He gets these projects started and then drops them when he loses interest. Sometimes I don't even know until afterwards, and then by accident, like when I was walking down a side street downtown one early evening on my way to scope out a new bar, Aunt Fred's, and what do I see in a storefront window? A polished headstone, a life-size example of what can be ordered from a mason, according to the sign, for under a thousand dollars. It rests on a nest of black velvet, and is elevated so that the inscription catches the eye.

Charles William Banta

At Rest

1919–1986

"Can I help you?" the clerk asks when I walk through the door. He's no more than twenty-five, Italian good-looking, dark eyes, and far enough away from death to sell it with a clear conscience. I circle the slab of granite.

"A fine piece of work," he encourages. His voice is deeper than you'd expect.

Either the name or the dates alone could be a coincidence, but both?

"Johnny," the young man identifies himself and holds out his hand for me to shake.

"Johnny," I say. "Charlie Banta is my dad."

Johnny, still grinning, tries to place the name. I nod toward the stone and watch him read.

"Oh, shit."

"Johnny, I've got to ask you: what's going on?"

He looks around for another customer, glances over at the phone to make sure it isn't ringing.

"I didn't do the sale," he says at last. "It happened before I started working here."

"But you know the story."

"I heard about it. This older guy—I mean, your father—comes in one day and orders a stone, for himself he claims. Wants top of the line, the best engraving. Makes a down payment of two hundred dollars, so the owner—Curtis?—goes ahead and places the order. It comes back a month later, we call the . . . your dad . . . and he says he's changed his mind. Curtis was totally pissed. Talked about small-claims court but it was too much of a hassle. So for revenge he sends the rock back to have the year of death carved in, then sticks it in the window. Sick, huh?"

It was Dad all over.

"Do you, does he, live in the neighborhood? I guess he'd be pretty upset to see it, but it's been here all this time, at least a year, and—"

"He hasn't seen it, and if he did, he'd laugh or want a commission for the use of his name," I say. Johnny in his embarrassment has developed a great blush, which makes him look even better. "And me, I'm on my way over to a place I heard about. Aunt Fred's?"

Johnny gives a half-smile, relieved and something more.

"I guess it's cool if you're still into disco."

"Not necessarily."

D EE DEE MUST HAVE JUST GOTTEN off the phone because she's there on the first ring.

"Doctor Anderson?"

"It's Don Banta," I tell her. "I represent Allied Pharmaceuticals."

"You're the one who gave me that sample for Jeremy."

I figure Jeremy must be the kid in the photo on her desk.

"The same."

"Amazing."

"What is amazing?"

"Mr. Banta, you may very well have saved my son's life this morning."

I had been leaning back against the pillows, but sit up straight at this announcement.

"He had an attack about four, the worst one ever. I used his old prescription, I patted his chest, but nothing helped. Finally I called 911 but while I was waiting for the ambulance his lips started to go blue and suddenly I remembered that inhaler and what you called it: a miracle worker. I needed a miracle. It was still in my purse."

"What happened?"

"What happened is it calmed him down." Dee Dee's voice is strained with exhaustion. "I can't believe you're calling me. It's like you knew."

"He's all right now?"

"Mr. Banta, my family owes you a big one. If ever—*if ever*—there's anything . . ."

I close my eyes and I feel the chain of things: Dad to me, me to Dee Dee, Dee Dee to her kid. There's purposes we don't suspect, side paths we don't venture but a few steps down, and yet there's a give-and-take that leads forward, a surprise when we don't even know we need it. For the first time in a while I remember I'm a part of the flow, more than I admit, a river that can best be witnessed from very far away.

"It's like you knew all along," Dee Dee repeats for the lack of anything else to add.

"I . . ." I begin, but then the words stick. My fingers curl tight around the receiver and I stare at my packed suitcase where it waits by the door.

"Are you there?" Dee Dee wants to know. "Hello? Mr. Banta?"

I don't answer, I don't have one thing to say, and after a moment, the line goes dead.

THE DARK SNAKE

WHEN ANDREW LEFT THAT
morning in the June of 1900 he called good-bye, but as
proof of mild annoyance I neglected to answer. His
voice, barely deepened at fifteen to that of a man, hung
loud in the air, mixing with the slam of the door. I
hummed to myself above the noise, and remained at
the table cleaning my ivory hairbrush. My hair's fine
blackness was my signature, the legacy of a shipwrecked
Spaniard off the Armada who fought the Irish Sea and
arrived, they say, bedraggled but preening, at the cot-

tage door of some great-grandmother. In every generation that followed, it is said, there was one like me. My mother used to call it a rain of Moorish silk as she brushed two hundred strokes before prayers. Never cut since birth, each wisp that pulled free I now collected and worked into a coil wound in a crystal salver, a dark snake that seemed to shift and expand through the cuts and engravings.

If I had looked up from my work, I might have watched Andrew walk down the lane, through the gate, but instead, I was content to see him then as I have had to do thereafter in clear imagination, as different from the rest of us as a bird to a school of fish. His small eyes are sharp sapphire jewels beneath a prominent brow, his shoulders knobby, his arms have outgrown the shirt I stitched only months before, his father's old tan shoes are tightly laced. He's proud, straining to be grown, alert to resent every request out of my mouth, no matter how reasonable. That day I stopped myself from saying, "Tame your yellow mop into a part and button your coat." I didn't ask where he was going and when he would return—useless questions, I had recently discovered. In my own resentment, I spoke not at all. I demanded respect.

From birth Andrew possessed a formality, a self-fascination, that required him to make announcements of his condition, of his pleasure or anguish, of his hunger or fatigue or good health. He reported on himself always, and as with the bulletins issued by starlings beyond the windows, I eventually ceased to pay notice. He was like a clock that chimes the hour, and so I failed to hear in that morning's departure the slowing time. Failed to hear, and yet hear even now, hear ever since, unless I plan distraction.

From this vantage of twenty years I see what I should have known. Robert was not only older brother but model, the decade dividing him and Andrew a perpetual impatience. For me, of course, the distance between the birth of my two sons, the first and the final of my children, seemed immense, a long closet filled with words. Conceived in my fortieth year, Andrew was the last hope I would cast into the world, the last advance before the long retreat I had witnessed so often in others and had prepared myself in Jesus to accept. He could never age in my eyes, never be other than a boy, impulsive and sweet.

So I paid too small attention to his interest in Robert's railroad work. I even made him a cap of striped ticking and a kerchief of red cotton, as if his ambition were nothing more than a costume fancy. I believed I had time to discourage his desire and forgot that not everyone saw my son through a mother's eyes. Those hiring agents must have been blind, must have observed him from behind, the outline of a man not yet inhabited. They took his word, they later claimed, they had no reason to doubt him, so tall and sure. They're sorry. They didn't know.

He must have gone directly to the station, for his first day he must have set his watch to be there on time to ride the eight o'clock. His job was to shovel coal into an open fire. Bent double, his clean clothes surely black-smudged in minutes, his sleeves not yet rolled, he could not have seen out that high vacant window that allowed a square of breeze into the car. He was a hard worker when he wanted to be and would have pushed to impress those men whose ranks he yearned to join. Dauntless in his strength, he would have looked no further beyond the mechanical motion of his shovel than to search the red shifting arc of ashes for a hollow nest in which to fit another load.

I was changing sheets, stuffing a pillow into an embroidered case fresh from the line, when I heard a knock, blunt as if a crow had clapped blind into the side of the house. It came again, and I descended the stairs, smoothing loose strands against my scalp, searching in my apron pocket for a hairpin. It was unusual to have an afternoon caller, and so I was unprepared.

"Mrs. William Burke?" asked a man in a black suit of clothes.

"I am."

"There's been a train accident." The lines in his face

deepened, underscoring his message. His eyes were not without pity, but curious.

"Robert!" I said, and reached behind to the banister for support.

The man shook his head. "It's the other one. The boy who started just this morning. It happened so fast."

I folded to the bottom step, watched his mouth.

"There was a cow on the tracks," he went on, as if this explained something. "Are you hearing me? A milk cow."

My mind in its denial flew anywhere and landed first in retort. *The train hit the cow, not the other way around,* I wanted to say. Yet this distinction was but temporary protection. I soon discovered anger as my shield, and then my sword.

"Do they pay you to dress up and bring bad news? Do they ask you when you return to that office that waged an underage boy how she took your message? Do they wonder if the mother cried before you, hid her hands in her skirts and covered her face?"

He shrank before my armor, his nervous thumbs misshaping the brim of his hat.

"We've taken the liberty of having the remains removed to Koster's," he said at last. "The casket must be closed, of course."

"Of course." My voice was the echo of itself.

"If there's anything I—or the company can do . . ."

I stood in answer to his stupid sympathy, to his pink skin blotched from the drink he needed to fortify himself before facing me. I closed the door without another word and studied the inset panels, wooden windows stained a lighter brown than pine, and counted on my moving fingers the ones whom I must inform. With each name I removed from my coiled hair a silver clip, and before I was done the famous braid hung below my waist, its weight pulling at the back of my neck, elevating the level of my vision.

I thought of shears. Let a cropped head speak for me. Let the smell of burning raven hair be incense for this empty house.

But such an act would be pure gesture, all show and no effect.

After some time, the door opened and Robert appeared framed by afternoon sunlight and the green blur of front yard trees stirred by wind. His throat was flushed with running, and his brown eyes were bright as creek stones. I waited while his breath slowed and did not help him find speech. I begrudged him the years he had lived beyond Andrew's age. I begrudged him his choice of job, his rapid promotion—so irresistible a beacon. I begrudged him the ability to stand upright. I begrudged his wholeness, his puny regret, his future, the pump of his healthy lungs.

"They've been here, then," he said, gathering his deduction from the sight of me. "I wanted you to hear it from my mouth, but I had no ride."

"It doesn't matter."

"It was a freak accident. A cow strayed from the field. It caught a hoof between the ties."

"Who told you?"

"The brakeman saw and threw the lever. The animal was never touched. The derailment was caused by the sudden stop, not by impact."

"Where is this cow? Who owns it?"

Robert shook his head as if to clear his thoughts, and pulled the end of his mustache with one hand.

"I think she was freed. She's gone home."

"And if this brakeman had done nothing? If he had driven into the cow? What then?"

"Her weight against the velocity of the train . . . it wouldn't have mattered much. A jolt to those on board."

I saw it clear, black and white as the picture shows in town each Friday evening. I watched the engine approach around a bend. The music of a piano rose. The cow pulled frantically, digging her hind legs into the gravel bed, twisting her horned head in effort. The whistle sounded, once, again, yet the turn of the wheels did not slacken. The cow's eyes rolled toward me, sapphire, sapphire, her thick muzzle moved to speak against the roar. All sight was lost in dust.

ANDREW WAS ALWAYS THE KIND who couldn't keep silent, who entrusted to me every passing thought, and that, I think, was the hardest part to bear. I missed his gossip, but worse, I could not drive from my mind the sureness that he was frustrated in his wish to confess his new experience. I listened deep within myself. I made my mind a white sheet ready for his ink. I honed my inner hearing the way I've seen fiddlers tune an instrument, running the notes through their extremes, eliminating discords until all that were left were the match to ideal memory, and then for an instant there would sound his voice, recognizable and distinct, forming words so much his own that my pulse signaled in reply. I'd catch fragments of sentences or the chorus of a summer church hymn, his pitch a familiar octave below my own, before it dappled.

"You'll never believe it," he began one morning just before the sun rose through my eastern window. And then he was gone.

"I saw . . ." he said another time, late, but the rest of the message was a shout from behind a jagged hill.

"Who?" I demanded back, piercing as a silent

thought can be. "Who did you see there? Aunt Katey? Your pappa?"

"Yes," I seemed to sense, with not a clue to which.

"Were they well-dressed? Are you peaceful in the Lord's embrace?"

I never spoke of these talks, not to my nieces who came to make pies and clean cupboards, not to prim-faced neighbors who ate iced cake on the front porch, not even to Robert, who was my strength throughout the wake. I desired no pamperings, no nods with eye-brows raised as though a mother's bereavement were the most familiar experience in the world. In private I hesitated before summoning the image of Andrew's face, as if that click of perfect vision I insisted upon achieving before I surrendered to sleep were in an ex-haustible supply. I feared to use up my ration of An-drew and so I parceled him as sparingly as fresh water on the boat from Ireland, once a day, and willed myself content.

Yet I hated his loneliness worse than my own. He was nailed in raw boards, stifled by packed earth, as dependent upon me for interpretation and words as he had been when, a helpless babe, I alone could read his thoughts. I knew to turn or change him, knew if he felt hot or chilled, knew the shape of his bad dreams and how to lullaby his fears. From the wreck of his delivery,

I sensed his moods the way they say a severed limb feels pain.

So now, when I heard his muffled demand for justice, could I stop my ears?

"I'm sorry," he always ended, but sorrow was too weak a dam.

There was but one enemy whose guilt was clear, and a single weapon at my disposal. It was enough. I knew my course the moment the railroad president offered money.

"There will be expenses, I'm sure," he said to me even before the soft ground over Andrew had been hardened by the first night's dew. "We feel somehow responsible because we didn't check his particulars."

He gave me an engraved card that bore his name and address, and the name of the railroad, in etched script, and I slipped it into my glove, against my palm. I caught his fear on my tongue and made no reply that he could hear.

All that week I went to daily Mass and remained kneeling when others stood or sat. The monsignor assumed that I prayed for Andrew and kept his eyes fixed on me during his blessings. He sensed me as he raised the chalice, as he broke the consecrated wafer and summoned the Savior. On Sunday he spoke of the loss the Father felt for the Son's sacrifice, and asked the congregation to ponder Mary, who never despaired that He would rise. Robert's nervous wife Alice, at my side in the pew, touched my glove at this homily lest I miss the parallel. I wore black tulle, my widow's mourning dress, and the skin of my arms gleamed beneath its shine. I draped net to conceal my eyes, which never closed except in blinks, and feigned to listen, but easy comfort was not my object. I used those hours of quiet to sort choices, to foresee the years that remained me. If I were to prevail, it would be through suffering.

The next week, still in my weeds, I walked to town, to the firm that drew my will, to Horace Wilton, who had read my husband's own testament eight years gone and was of a family connected through marriage to mine. His wall was hung with parchment diplomas, each framed in thin blond wood and protected by glass. He stood like a gentleman when I entered his rooms, ushered me to his oaken desk, and waited on me before seating himself, placing his hands palms-down upon his blotter.

"Rebecca," he said. "It is God's tragedy, but a mercy that he went so quickly."

"I'm not here to talk of that," I replied. His fingernails were clean, squared by a file.

"Well, then. If there's something else. How may we assist you?"

I opened my purse and extracted its solitary content.

"Ingersoll's card," Horace Wilton read and looked at me, confusion in his brow.

"Sue them," I said. "Ruin them."

He removed his rimless glasses one ear at a time, shook his head. "If there's a question of liability, I'm sure we can reach a proper settlement. I know how badly those boys feel. I'm confident recompense can be arranged without resort to courts of law."

"It's not money I desire."

Horace squinted, seemed to see me in my gathered purpose, and scraped back his chair. "Have you considered carefully?" he asked in a shocked voice. "Have you discussed this move with Robert?"

"It is not his affair."

"But surely you realize that it will be Robert who bears the consequence. If you should embarrass the railroad it is his career in jeopardy."

I knew this, but I was not interested. Robert could protect himself, and at any rate, what kind of man would work in the employ of his brother's murderers?

"There are other jobs," I said.

"He's a married man with two daughters, your grandchildren. He can't just walk away. He's given them seven years."

"A small number against a life."

"He is your son as well," Horace Wilton protested.

I asked myself, then answered aloud, the only mother's question that mattered. "I would do the same for him."

THE DAY THE WRIT WAS SERVED Robert came to beg.

"I wouldn't ask for myself, Mama, but I will for Alice and the girls."

I reached out my hand to him. His eyes were dull, full of the knowledge that his plea was useless. "There must be a balance to things. Were I to let Andrew go so peacefully as they wish, his life is forfeit, a thing not worth a weekly paycheck. Without a counterweight he is forgotten. Without my voice the cow becomes the story: 'The cow who caused a train wreck and, oh yes, I think a boy was killed. *But the cow lived.*' A tale odd enough to be retold, and always the boy will have no name."

Robert sat on my plush couch, bent forward, his head low, but he listened.

"It must be different." I rapped my knuckles on my knee. "The story will be instead that Andrew Burke and his martyrdom brought down a railroad. You can't deny your brother that."

Robert looked up, resentment coloring his voice. "I

grieve him too, Mama. You're not alone in responsibility, not the center of the world. But why add more sadness? This tale, that cow and our Andrew, will have escaped human memory in fifty years. Don't imagine our lives matter past their limit."

"Then what I do, I do for *me,*" I said. "For *me,* if that's the only way you can understand. Tell that to your Alice and let her complain. But ask how she would avenge her daughters, ask if there are boundaries."

Robert stood, his back to me, and buttoned his coat.

"She said it was hopeless because Andy was your youngest."

"My love is equally distributed." I dared him to meet my eyes. But he wouldn't turn.

"Not to the living. Survival makes us invisible. Do you assume you are a mystery behind your veils? You think only how you failed to keep Andy. But imagine your fury if he were only injured. He lied to you. He deceived you. They say if the fire in the box had been less high that the train might have stopped more gently. It's true. It's accident that he's gone, but not that he left. Andy was so in need to come back to this house a man and therefore to leave it—oh, I remember that need—that he piled the coal to overflowing, stoked the furnace beyond its limit. The engine was at

183

racing heat, Mama, out of control. If there is blame, share it."

I left Robert where he stood, crossed the carpet on feet that trod so heavily they left impressions, and climbed the stairs. I turned the lock in my room and sat on the edge of the bed and didn't relax the muscles of my neck until I heard the front door open, creak, then firmly close.

I<small>T ALL HAPPENED AS PREDICTED.</small> I won a settlement of two thousand dollars and spent it every penny on a granite monument for Andrew's grave. It is a thing of beauty, a sight for all who visit. A mail-clad angel stands guard above the carved words: "Not Gone." The railroad was dealt a blow and in return Robert lost his position. He and Alice and my two young granddaughters went to Louisville, where he took itinerant work in the mills. I heard they've moved three times since.

But I am not lonely. Once as I sat on my porch working tangles from my braid a limping stranger paused before my gate. He carried a red valise and leaned on a polished wooden crosier for support.

"Hello," he waved. "I cannot help but notice your hair. I've seldom seen the like of it."

I never ceased the sweep of my arm. I was heavy by

then, filled the seat of my rocker, yet I felt renewed in his vision.

In times now past there was a steady stream of such men, ready to sell you potions or capture you in a photograph, tinkers and gypsies looking for cool drink. This wanderer reminded me of another who knocked at our door the summer Andrew was six. For a price he promised us immortality, our posed image recorded for all who came after. Long minutes in the heat we had to hold perfectly still, my husband and me sitting side by side, each bounded by a son. The insects were terrible, I remember, stinging and buzzing while we were frozen.

"Your hair," the crippled man repeated, and shifted his weight. "How did you come by it?"

"I take no credit for the Lord's blessing," I answered honestly, but I knew what he meant. Soon after the verdict of that juried trial, the new growth changed. Not to white, as you might expect in a woman of fifty-six years, but to purest gold. More remarkable than that, whole tresses seemed to alter overnight, from root to end, and by the time a year had passed the transformation was complete. Wherever I went I was pointed out, the subject of awe and conversation. There were those who asked for a lock, for luck, they said, but really it was for the oddness.

"It's amazing," the man said. He wanted an invitation to sit, to share the shade of my roof, and contrived flattery. "Have you ever thought of going on the stage? In a carnival? It's that unusual. Angel hair crowning an old woman."

He meant his words as compliment, no doubt of that, but I stopped my chair all the same. "There's work to be done," I said, and waited him out. In a moment he continued on his way. Thereafter, in public I covered my head with a shawl.

B UT AT HOME, ILLUMINATED BY the kerosene lamp that stands by the mirror next to the bolted front door, I comb the length of each strand with my spread hand, counting, weighing, and tell endlessly of the day's events. In the cascade that spills over my shoulders, down my arms, and over my breast, I address and scold him in luxury—he whom no one else has recognized in its brazen shade.

The photograph is yellow too, spotted with dried water, bent at the edges, but not a night passes that I don't read its surface with my fingers. All that persists of my husband's head is a burst of light, a candle glow without flame. Behind him Robert stands as if obscured by a blowing gauze curtain. But due to some accident of paper the left side of the print is intact, clear as the day it was made. I am dark and Andrew fair, and we frown with identical expressions. His hand on my shoulder is covered with my own. In the tumble of years he has returned again to that compliant age, and so remains.

The house fills with sounds, with quick footsteps on the stairs, with babies' cries, with the share of grace before meals, and I talk into the early morning about little things, trifles hardly worth a mention. My voice carries strong to every corner, seals each window crack, awakens the fire. Sometimes we sing.

Oui

Now I won't say I always live my life by dreams, but I do cherish them when they come to me, and I do try to act on them whenever practical. The challenge is: unless I commit their messages to paper the minute I wake up, they blow away like letters set on the grass. It's as though the words are traced in spit, and I don't dare allow them to dry out. I'll click a ballpoint pen, turn my room upside down for a scrap to write on, but by the time I'm ready to record, usually all I know for sure is that I've forgotten something good. I spend those mornings almost retrieving it, dancing up to it from this angle or that to tease it into clear focus, but it hovers just beyond my reach.

Such days don't come along often, thank God, but when they do, they usually turn out to be special—inspired almost. Should a surprising possibility present itself, I generally leap, abandoning caution and good sense. I say accidents won't happen under the guidance of your own voice, vague as it might be, so why not plunge in?

Of course, this line of argument has resulted in a career path that might appear, to someone who doesn't understand the source of its inspiration, less than a straight shot from A to B. I started out ordinary enough, a plowboy from western Montana, outside Polson, a loner not entirely by choice. When the other guys were off partying or running around, I was bucking bales. I drove a pickup when I was six, after my uncle fixed it so I could stand up and operate the pedals. Once a cop stopped me, looked me over, shook his head, then proceeded on. He could tell I was competent, for my age.

In high school I played center. I was strong from all that hauling and could snap the ball then take out one, two opponents, even occasionally break through to the backfield without breathing hard. Ronan put three against me one time, and that slowed me down, yet they knew I was there by the second half when I creamed the tight end. Technically what I did was illegal. You're supposed to fall with your man but I just picked him up and pile drived him home. He made a sound I can still hear—like a tire blowing. The officials backed the ambulance directly onto the forty-yard line and everyone in the bleachers gave a standing ovation when they sirened out the guy. In the locker room after the game we heard the damage report: two broken ribs and a dislocated collarbone. He was lost for the season. The coach shook his head, said, "I told you, shake him up, ice him for one, two plays. But jeez, Dwayne . . ." He was trying his best not to grin.

I joined the service, reenlisted twice for lack of a better idea, but when my last two-year hitch in Germany was over, I decided it was time to get on with whatever. The only hiring I could find near Polson, though, was in timber. You might know it was the summer of '84 when the average temperature was ninety-five in town, add ten or fifteen degrees out where we were stumping. "Break your ass in the morning when it's cool," the boss advised us. "Take it easy in the afternoons." That was his big mistake, because we didn't do diddley after that. It was so hot we stripped down to our shorts, got covered with dirt dry as powder. Even so, I changed my clothes every day when we'd stop off for a cool one at the bar and café Mom had opened after Dad passed away.

I tried cooking for her the next fall, but it was a no go. She was too particular—everything had to have the homemade touch. When we opened at six, the truckers expected their sticky buns, and four full trays would be gone by ten o'clock. Most nights Mom would keep me in the kitchen till midnight, getting ready for the next day's specials. Probably that's what cut short her life at sixty-two, that attitude of nothing but the best. If she were me now, she'd probably be listening to Berlitz language tapes every night, probably know more grammar than your average Frenchman—but I'm getting ahead of the story.

When she gets pissed, Cecille accuses me of being with her just to escape work I didn't like, of trading one short-order job for another, but that's not so. I chose for the prospect of love, was sunk for keeps the day she stopped into the café side and ordered a Denver omelet. She was wearing a two-piece flowery dress, her brown hair was windblown and wild and—I can't quite explain it—she cleared a space around herself with the force of her personality. I couldn't resist to inquire about her ultimate destination.

She was heading west alone, she told me, on the scenic route to be an assistant day manager at the Moses

Lake Resort and Convention Center. Her Corolla was packed so high that she could only see behind by using the side mirrors—and the right one was tough for her to negotiate. She admitted that she'd barely avoided catastrophe in downtown Dickinson, North Dakota, where she had been forced to parallel park.

Wouldn't you know it? All that very morning one of those strong-impression dreams had been slipping through my fingers. All the hours I'd been wiping counters, stacking plates, ringing up checks, I was mentally coaxing and squinting. "Louder," I had told my memory six times a minute. "Speak up."

"Looks to me like you need a man to ride shotgun," I joked, making conversation when Cecille told me of her problem.

"The seat's empty so I guess you could say the position's open."

To my amazement she sounded as though she could be serious. I looked into her eyes and she didn't flinch away. We fired wordless questions and answers back and forth, the equivalent of: "No!" "Really!" "Really?" "Well . . ." "Oh." "Yes." "Yes?" "Yes." "Okay." "Okay." Our debate was like a dropped saucer settling on the floor, first one side up then the other, but finally it stabilized for me, the weight of my previous night's dream playing a significant factor.

Cecille waited while I gathered up my belongings,

which luckily weren't many because I had to hold them on my lap for the next ten hours.

"I can't explain it," I told Mom. "So I won't even try. You'll have to bake all the rolls yourself for tomorrow."

"I did it solo before you showed up and God knows I can again," were her parting words to me. Her years operating a highway establishment had long ago turned my mother philosophical about the unpredictability of comings and goings.

"I halfway know why I'm sitting here," I said to Cecille once we were heading south on Highway 93, "but what's your excuse for letting me?"

She glanced over her shoulder automatically, no doubt asking herself the same thing, then turned her attention back to the highway. "I've tried everything else. Blind dates. Answering ads in the personals. I'm tired of waiting for Prince Charming—no offense. You . . ." She was going to add something more but stopped herself, drew a breath, flicked a look in my direction. "You were more than generous with your chopped bell peppers." She nodded twice, slowly. "I took that as a positive sign."

CECILLE THOUGHT SHE COULD GET me on in janitorial or maintenance, me being so big, but the resort was already fully staffed. She got to live in the expense-paid junior administrator's suite, which, to free up an extra room for tourists, was time-shared with the assistant night manager. The big disadvantage to this deal was that Cecille had to be up and gone, some-place, by seven A.M. because, as you might expect, Lewis—that was the guy's name—was dead on his feet at the end of his shift. It was in her contract that the sheets had to be changed and the bathroom cleaned up by the time her counterpart knocked on the door for his turn.

It also turned out to specify in the fine print that Moses Lake employees could not entertain in their rooms members of the opposite sex from themselves, unless the person was a relative. That left us with a major housing dilemma: between us we couldn't raise a security deposit for a private apartment, and I wasn't exactly easy to conceal. That first week I spent my nights as a paying guest in a single—at least I had the benefit of Cecille's influence with the reservation clerk and therefore enjoyed a view of the lake—and Cecille came up to visit as her schedule permitted. Then, on the last morning before my severance check from Mom ran out, I mercifully woke up with my head full of dream. I reached for the complimentary pencil and the handy pad of Moses Lake Resort notepaper and jotted down: *There's a man and a woman standing on a sticky*

194

bun, their feet planted in the icing. A dog goes by with a fish in its mouth.

I don't claim every dream is simple to decipher, or that I can immediately put into effect every specific point, but there was no mistaking that breakfast roll, plain as a three-tiered cake. When Cecille telephoned to give me my wake-up call, I told her I believed we were destined to get married, and we might as well do it sooner rather than later to save another night's charges. She could see the convenience and financial logic of my plan, but to tell you the truth I don't think she believed me when I told her how the idea had originated.

"There's no necessity to make up excuses," she told me. "A simple 'I love you and can't go on without you' will do."

"Well, that too," I said.

Living with Mom, I had learned when to shut up and let the other person define a situation.

M OSES LAKE HAS THE FEEL OF A movie I once saw about life in a Martian space colony: an outpost, all built up at the same time from prefab components, on the edge of nothing identifiable. To the north, the brown desert of central Washington sweeps toward the Cascade range, and to the south is the shore of the blue lake created when the Columbia was dammed. The climate is dry and the sky is cloudless, visibility unlimited—perfect for training exercises.

Most mornings our alarm clock is the unmistakable rumble of a jumbo jet, high up waiting its turn. Seven days a week, chances are you can look out the window and a 747 will break into sight, broad wings dipping right, then left, nose aimed at the earth, engine coughing. The logo on the side might be a red sun, a new moon and star, a long green sword with Arab-looking writing underneath. I imagine a pilot shouting into his radio, his eyes bright with adrenaline, his hands reaching for control buttons as he tries to follow instructions memorized from a manual and previously practiced only on a computer simulator. The descent is steep, the sound blankets the ground, and I can't help it: even in the security of my own bedroom, I duck.

People around here are used to ignoring terror from above. Nobody cheers when the turbines kick in, when the jets find air to balance on, when a plane safely heads back to the far corner of the former air force base, now rented out to foreign airlines. It's all just so much noise pollution compensated by the extra revenues that keep property taxes low. Flight crews have to practice emergency procedures somewhere, the booster feeling goes, and Moses is damn lucky to be it.

As a kind of perk, most everybody in town gets

offered a free scenic ride—"an aerial view of the oasis" —complete with at least one guaranteed emergency. I suspect that controlling passenger behavior in a panic situation is just another test cabin attendants have to pass. You take off, then wait for a red warning flash, hear the pilot's calm voice come on in a Spanish or Korean accent and tell you to lean forward, protect your head. I thought the drill was a kick myself, the time we went, and played along. I turned to Cecille and said, "It's been a great life, darling, thanks to you." But her face was white and her jaw muscles were flexed, so I put my hand on top of hers where it gripped the armrest and didn't say another word until we were back on the ground.

"I've found out a very important fact about myself," she told me as she fastened her seat belt for the drive home. "I hate to fly. You couldn't pay me a thousand dollars to leave the earth again."

I SCOUTED AROUND FOR WEEKS, inquiring into this or that career opportunity. Now that I was her responsibility, Cecille took me in hand and typed a resumé to equip me for each job description I picked up at unemployment. On a Monday I might be an expert carpenter, the following Wednesday an experienced insurance claims adjuster. I kept watching for a pastry chef's slot to open up, knowing that I could impress them with the skills I learned from Mom, but the food-service market was glutted with part-timers from the local community college.

Then one morning while we were reading the paper together in the lobby, as we did every day to kill time before the early checkouts, Cecille spied two items in the classifieds that were to change my life. The first was for an emergency fill-in modern language instructor at Big Bend High School, and the second was for a two-year-old purebred apricot toy poodle, which was offered for free to a good home. Pets "within reason" were allowed at the resort, and Lewis said he didn't mind since he needed company in the afternoons, so Cecille dialed the dog first.

"Remember the fish," she reminded me, wiggling her eyebrows to head off any possible objections. She was not above exploiting my dreams when they corresponded with her ambitions.

The couple who owned Coco was splitting up and couldn't decide who got to take custody. Both of them were sentimental because they had named him after their favorite cereal, Cocoa Puffs—and from what I could tell when they came over, that joint taste was about the only thing they had in common. The idea was, they were supposed to drop off Coco for a trial visit, but when they showed up with his little bed and his toys and his bowl, I knew it was for keeps. The minute I saw him, I thought "Uh oh," and sure enough for Cecille it was chopped green peppers all over again. That same afternoon I made an appointment with the high school, though I didn't hold out much hope, since the only French I ever personally attempted was during short military leaves on the Riviera—"yes," "no," "how much?" "thanks a lot." Not exactly a language lab.

The principal was a man named Mr. Simms, a naturally nervous type. I could tell my size put him into a state, but being the head honcho, he tried not to show it.

"So, Dwayne," he said, perusing the current version of my resumé. I hadn't bothered to read this one myself, figuring it was better to know too little rather than too much when you didn't in fact know anything at all. "You speak French, do you?"

"Oui," I answered.

"You've studied abroad?"

"Oui."

"And you're new to Moses Lake but your credentials are coming airmail."

"Oui. Merci."

I had to hand it to Cecille. I shifted my weight, and the wood of the chair gave a loud groan. Mr. Simms sat up straighter.

"Do you, ah, have any additional skills?" he wanted to know.

I thought for a minute.

"Oui," I said, and allowed in English as how I could probably coach football on the side. I told him about the time with the tight end, and Mr. Simms was suddenly on full alert.

"Excellent." He nodded when I was done, and the job was mine, starting on Monday. He directed me to the Humanities Department, where I picked up the textbook and the grade sheet that the previous French teacher had left behind after the second week of fall term when she ran off to Seattle with a senior. I met the woman who taught Spanish, but she didn't have much to say once I answered "Very," to her "Married?"

"What's she look like?" Cecille asked when I related the story, then lost interest when I pointed at Coco, who was sitting on her lap, the position he tended to occupy from that day forward.

I WAS ASSIGNED TO TEACH FRENCH 1, 2, and 3, and 3 was the one that worried me. The way I saw it, by the time I started I could be four days up on 1, not far behind on 2, but would be left at the gate when fifth period rolled around.

"Why did you sign up for this course?" I asked a girl in the front row, to break the ice. It was *deux heures de l'après-midi,* and I felt like this was the opening play of a big game in which I was a distinct underdog.

"The magazines," she informed me, and pulled out an issue of *Vogue* in French—at least I assumed that was what it was in. "I want to be a cosmetologist and the models give me ideas for new styles."

That explained her hair.

I had previously put the same question to a boy in 2, and he'd shut his eyes.

"Get real, dude. Consider the alternative."

Which was, I later found out, something called "Hands-on Masterpieces of Spanish Drama," a subject in which my competing language instructor held an M.A. degree.

So I was heading for a touchdown, or would have been except for Rhonda Stevenson. I heard trouble ahead when she introduced herself.

"Gemma Pell Hwonda." She frowned.

I admired her at first, assuming she had a speech impediment, but then I realized that she was possibly speaking French and expected me to answer in kind.

"*Oui,*" I said.

Rhonda was not fooled, and reeled off another string of yap-yap-yap before she took her seat, picked up her pencil, and waited to learn something.

"Just don't call on her," Cecille advised that night. We were snuggled up as usual on the clean sheets Lewis had left us. "I know the type. They always want in-room coffee and wake-up calls at odd hours, seven-seventeen or something. The only way to survive is to ignore them."

We were watching *Terminator 2* for the third time. Thanks to Cecille's job we got to see all the closed-circuit shows we wanted, for free. She especially liked the ones with violence, since she could pretend she was offing troublesome guests. Even as we spoke, Arnold Schwarzenegger was shooting a security guard in the knees. "Room 209," Cecille said. "Bloody nose all over the sheets. A party that claimed to be from Boise, Idaho. Die."

I didn't encourage these fantasies since sooner or later my name would likely appear on Cecille's list. I hoped it wouldn't be when the next *Alien* movie came out. Cecille strongly identified with the Sigourney Weaver character.

"Rhonda won't put up with that," I told her. "She'll bitch."

"To who, the wimpoid principal?" Cecille's eyes were fixed on the TV screen. Every now and then she'd whisper "Pow," under her breath.

"To him, yes," I said. "But that's not what really

bugs me. The next thing I know she'll be organizing bake sales to pay for a class trip to France."

That's exactly what happened.

I was left out of the loop on a lot of the plans since Rhonda insisted on giving her progress reports in French, but I didn't worry too much because there was no way in hell she could raise that kind of cash. Let the French Club peddle their *"pâtisseries"* on long tables at the entrance to Rosauer's grocery store. Let them spend their Saturdays, dressed as clowns or hookers in fishnet hose, washing cars. The furthest the proceeds would take them was to Calgary, where nobody spoke any more *français* than I did.

Of course, I hadn't factored in Air France wanting to keep up public relations with the population of Moses Lake. I guess they worried that if they got kicked out here, their new pilots would have to practice swan dives over their own country, so it was cheaper to play along with community spirit. When the local rep, a *Monsieur* Saint, heard about Rhonda's plan—from Rhonda, who else?—in no time flat he arranged for complimentary round-trip coach transportation—the whole French 3 class plus *le maître*, me—Moses Lake to Paris, for eight days and seven nights of culture. All we had to pay for were meals and lodgings, and those at a greatly reduced cost.

"Now what the fuck am I supposed to do?" I asked Cecille. "They're going to expect me to know what's what over there."

"Bring me back some cologne," she said. "And a scarf with some designer's name on it, I don't care whose."

"I may not come back," I said. "They'll probably stick my head in a guillotine."

"Hey, you can always wow them with your cinnamon rolls."

W<small>E</small> WERE SCHEDULED TO, AS Rhonda put it, day-par from Moses, connect to big planes in Seattle and New York, and arrive overseas by dawn the next day, something called "transfers" included. When we came back after a week, we'd arrive an hour before we left, thanks to the time zones. It was all worked out that we'd go to museums, take a boat ride where we'd eat our dinner, and hop a bus to see some king's palace, which was apparently located out of town. I kept thinking of that old song, "Please Mr. Custer, I Don't Want to Go."

"Will you stop humming?" Cecille could hardly wait for a vacation from me. I had driven her crazy with my worries, and she had started spending her evenings "out," as she put it. Where was "out" in Moses

Lake? It had to cross my mind that she might be seeing someone—I was that bad company. And I admit it, her secrecy took its toll on my emotions. I hated to lose the spark between us over the stress of a foreign language. Of course, instead of confessing my true feelings, I took them out on Cecille when she didn't show enough sympathy for my situation.

"Who saw the damn ad anyway?" I accused one day. "I ought to clear out of this town before the truth catches up to me."

Cecille was combing Coco while I practiced a *discours* about getting to and from a train station, and both woman and poodle turned toward me with the same hard-to-read expression.

"Quit your bellyaching," Cecille snapped. "If you get tripped up, claim those people speak a different brand of French than you learned. Make *them* the dummies. I do it all the time with guests who give me trouble over the charges from their minibars. Or just don't say anything. Let them wonder."

"You mean like when a person takes off in the evening and won't tell where she's been when somebody asks her?"

"I have a right to my life, Dwayne. We've been through this." Cecille got busy with a tangle behind Coco's ear.

"I can't exactly sell they don't speak French in

France," I protested, back to the crisis at hand. "Rhonda will report the shit out of me."

"So push her off the side of that restaurant boat," Cecille suggested. "Nobody'll miss a big mouth. Her parents will probably thank you. Just for God's sake don't run away from another thing in your life."

I F THE FOOTBALL TEAM MADE THE state tournament, which meant knocking off Wenatchee, I'd have no choice but to stay with my boys, see them through. Our chances for the playoffs weren't great, all things being equal, so I taught the defense every dirty move I ever knew, and they respected me for it.

Mr. Simms joined me to survey the practice field one afternoon in mid-November. He was a good foot shorter than me.

"I've been meaning to talk to you," he said. "Haven't you received my messages?"

He was still waiting for my transcripts and recommendations, and there were only so many times I could claim they had been lost in the mail.

"We've got a shot." I changed the subject, gestured toward a line of players who were taking turns running into a padded pole. "Hurt yourself," I yelled to encourage them.

"Wouldn't that be marvelous?" Mr. Simms kind of looked off into the distance, where a Korean Airlines plane was taking aim at a butte. "A trophy in the display case would put Moses Lake on the map. Make them take notice."

I didn't know who "they" were, but I agreed with him.

"Oui."

"I'm counting on you, Dwayne. We all are."

Okay. You'd think that someone who had lived for almost forty years would have heard a compliment like that often enough before, but if you did, you'd think wrong. Praise took me all the way back to high school.

"I won't let you down."

"Not just me. The whole community."

The whole community.

"Trust me," I said, another first.

After that, the drills were hell. I made the guys take extra laps, do two hundred sit-ups. I drew chalk diagrams on the blackboard till their eyes crossed. On my own time, I scouted Wenatchee's next two games and identified their weak spots, pinpointed the players they couldn't do without.

"You're possessed," Cecille decided, back late again without an excuse or an apology. "Possessed by the devil. All that violence. I don't know you at all."

"That about makes us even," I told her.

FINALLY THE BIG SATURDAY AR-
rived, and I took it as a good omen that the night
before I had a dream I could only partially remember. *I
see a triangle,* I had jotted down at dawn. *Orange. Maybe
more red than orange. The points are sharp. Johnny Carson is
wearing his turban.*

I knew there was more. I was positive Johnny Carson had told me something I had meant not to forget,
and I convinced myself that it was victory. After all,
one of the school's colors was red, and the triangle
could be a kind of loving cup, the type of thing they
engraved and presented to the winning coach.

If we beat Wenatchee, we played Skohokum in a
week's time for the State Double A Championship. If
we lost, I landed in France on Monday, so optimism
was my best card.

"It's up to you," I told my boys. "The eyes of the
world are on you. For better or worse, you'll remember
today for the rest of your lives—take it from me—so
make it for better." The team clasped their hands together and said, *"Yeah,"* then ran out onto the floodlit
field, growling and clapping.

Halfway through the longest last quarter of my life,
the scoreboard showing an impossible-to-overcome
44–3, I stared hard at the bleachers to see if Cecille had
shown up after all as a gesture of support, but I couldn't

penetrate the glare. From the bench, though, I did notice Mr. Simms talking to one of the school board members, and neither one of them was a bit entertained. Even some of the guys acted as though the humiliating defeat was my fault, especially the two of them who got booted from the game for unnecessary roughness.

I got home to a dark room and just inside the door was my suitcase, all packed and zipped for France with a Post-it from Cecille on the side. "I may be late but I'll see you in the morning."

I dialed Lewis at the front desk. "What time did she leave?"

"I couldn't tell you." His voice was tight with knowing more than he planned to reveal. "I'm in the middle of a group check-in."

S OMETIMES THERE'S SUCH A STRING of bad that you can't help but push for the end of it. You wait for the next blow because you know when you've absorbed them all at least they'll be behind you, so I did something I'm not proud of: I looked through Cecille's private things for some clue as to what was going down.

In her checkbook I found seventeen stubs, each a week apart and made out to "cash" in the amount of thirty-five dollars. In the wastebasket I discovered part of a letter from the people who owned the resort, granting Cecille an unpaid leave of absence—beginning the very day I was supposed to take off—even though she had been an employee for less than a year. And covered with a blanket, pushed far beneath our bed, I found a suitcase I had never seen before, locked and heavy. That was the clue that said it all, the one that sent me back to the car and kept me driving all night.

I would have thought Cecille had the class to dump me in person, though I couldn't blame her for leaving a phony, a loser whose adult life was one long hike downhill. But without her to come home to, why should I make myself miserable by going through with this stupid trip? What would those kids think of me two weeks from now if they had found themselves stranded in France with nobody but me to translate their basic needs? In Moses Lake I could fake it, be *Monsieur* Ballard, connoisseur of things *cher,* exhibitor of Impressionistic Art—just *regard* the posters on the walls of my classroom. Here, I could eat Sara Lee croissants and drink instant Old Vienna *café au lait,* but overseas? Overseas I'd be dumber than they were, yet another role model disappointment. No, as I crisscrossed the back roads of Grant County, waiting for the sun to rise, I decided that I had no choice but to come clean. Better to get the music over with here, where at least I was only a bus ride to my next stop. I'd leave a forwarding address for Cecille to send the papers.

T HE AIRPORT WAITING ROOM WAS packed: excited teenagers with backpacks at their feet, their parents looking on, worried but proud, brothers and sisters either bored or jealous. *Monsieur* Saint from Air France was in the middle of it all, getting his picture taken with Rhonda for the Spokane *Spokesman-Review*'s travel section.

I hadn't changed out of my coaching outfit, still had the whistle on a string around my neck. I hadn't shaved, hadn't stopped at the house because I didn't want to run into Cecille or find out that she was already gone.

"Alors, enfin, il arrive," *Monsieur* Saint cried out, and everybody turned to gawk at me. I opened my mouth, but before I could say word one, there was Cecille at my side, dressed up, lugging my suitcase in one hand and her own in the other.

"You scared the shit out of me," she said under her breath, and then in a normal voice she spoke confidently to the crowd.

"Unfortunately, my husband has lost his voice. *La voix de mon mari est perdue.*"

"That's a good one," I whispered back to her. "But they'll never go for it when . . ." Then it dawned on me what I had just heard her do. "You talked French."

The faces on the group of people all around us had gone blank. You could see them wondering, as if the words were in little cartoon clouds over their heads, *What does this news mean about the trip?*

"Not to worry," Cecille went on in her public ad–dress voice, *"Ça va.* Because I'm coming along and will be the tour guide until he's better. I'm trained in the language."

"You're what?"

"Don't strain your vocal cords, honey." Cecille bore down on every syllable and pinched my side for em–phasis. "You know what the doctor said. It's enough you pushed yourself against his advice and coached last night. Now you've got to give your throat a complete rest for a minimum of thirty-six hours."

The first boarding announcement came over the loudspeaker, and as the flashes of a dozen cameras went off and camcorders whirred, some students started moving toward the security check.

"But what if we had beat Wenatchee?"

That got me a look. "I've seen your team play, Dwayne, and anyhow, when did you ever stay in a place when you had the option to go?"

"Coco?"

Cecille deposited our bags on the conveyor belt to be X-rayed. "Kennel."

She smelled like perfume, like a scented coupon you'd find stuck between the pages of a glossy magazine. "Why didn't you tell me you knew French?"

"I just learned it," she said. "Surprised? I put an ad in the paper and found a private tutor over in Ephrata. When you didn't come home last night I thought I'd have to spend my overdue honeymoon in a single bed."

She handed over my passport, my tickets, my pocket dictionary, and an envelope full of medical release forms, then gave me a little shove toward the gate. "I'm right behind you."

"How much could you know?"

"How much do I need? Travel stuff, hotel stuff, food stuff. 'Where's the john?' Anything else, we'll wing it or make the students talk. Tell them it's a test or something." She patted her tote bag. "I brought along my practice tapes. You can bone up on the plane."

"Wait a minute." I held my ground, turned her toward me. "You're afraid to fly."

She couldn't deny it. There were panic lines around her mouth and the muscles of her arms were steel cables beneath my fingers. All the smart-ass jokes we usually piled between us, all the kidding around, the

lame alibis we each invented to explain our being together, staying together, had deserted her. Cecille stood
before me with no protective cover.

"There are things I'm scared of worse," was all she
said.

But it was all she had to say. Hearing those words,
I've got to tell you: it was as though in one burst every
last dream thought I had failed to drag into the light of
day flashed out in pure, legible neon—orange and red
and every other color you could possibly think to
name.

LAYAWAY

I WAS AT WAR FOR A FULL YEAR and never saw an enemy. I served my time in the Da Nang PX, dispensing gifts of guilt and love for belated birthdays, wedding anniversaries, and like occasions. Over time I became something of an expert on the cost required, discount or retail, to mend hurt feelings or to demonstrate a precise degree of affection. There were many factors to consider: ethnic group, age, married or not, and, of course, order of magnitude. For instance, was a present late because of forgetfulness or because of some other, less innocent excuse? That could spell a difference between a tape recorder without a built-in microphone and one with.

I had no prior experience as a store clerk, and had enlisted on impulse without the provision of promises. The army had no obligation to train me as a communications specialist or a machinist, and perhaps that very lack of designation, that space next to the line labeled "duty," was what sifted me into a role without a numbered category. My resumé in those days, if I had ever tried to record my life on the single side of a blank page, would have been distinguished only by my business diploma and my election, in my junior year, as secretary of the accounting club. Otherwise, I was normal.

I was born into a family that watched the highest-rated TV programs, that followed each new fad without the loyalty of a backward glance, that rooted for the home team in every seasonal sport. We voted for the winning ticket in elections, ate out at McDonald's slightly more often than at Burger King, wore green on St. Patrick's Day. We went to church on the holidays that required greeting cards, stayed home together on New Year's Eve, playing Monopoly until the ball dropped and Guy Lombardo struck up the band.

When I drew a low selective service number there was no doubt but that I would enlist. Why wait for the bus when you can walk? I had seen on the news, of course, about some who went to jail or to Canada but those weren't options for people like me. Dodging could ruin your life, and besides, Dad had served in France and Italy. He was on the phone all night bragging about his patriotic son the day I put my signed papers on the supper table for dessert.

I don't know what he told his clients when I was assigned to sales. Probably that ours was not to reason why, one of his favorite sayings, or that there were no unimportant jobs if done well, which was another. Maybe, Like father, like son. I personally took a certain amount of grief from other G.I.'s, not that most of those guys wouldn't have traded dog tags with me in a minute.

"Oh, man, what a fucking cush," my customers from infantry or armored would accuse as they rested their elbows on my counter, as they leafed through the catalog binder and made their selections from its laminated pages. Money was less a concern than the calculation of cost and intended message. Did a thirty-five-millimeter camera with built-in flash promise too much? Did a Sony Trinitron overstate with a twenty-one-inch diagonal screen, say, what might more accurately be conveyed with a thirteen-inch? Toilet water, cologne, or perfume? Domestic or imported?

They often asked my advice, painted a detailed

217

scene of where and to whom the item would be delivered, and I gave each purchase the benefit of my experience. Who knew the real stories? Who could distinguish gifts to wives and mothers from those that paid for services rendered? Some boys hoarded, accumulated boxes in their rooms back home in accord with their expected futures, and some bought as if tomorrow was behind them, like today was all that counted. My job was not to judge. Though I received no commission, I came to feel a certain proprietorship, to support one brand over another, to urge a man to spend a few dollars in order to buy a product that would last.

I had learned the tricks of subtle emphasis from watching my dad, who managed a Dodge dealership. There's no such thing as impulse, he once advised me. It's all in the display, the comparison. He decided a year in advance which models would move, and stocked those in quantity. The purchaser came in to be convinced, and there was nothing wrong in that, nothing sly. Who dealt in volume, after all? Who had read the fine print, the specifications? Dad respected his customers. He was doing them a favor by steering them in the right direction.

There were some soldiers I'd see each payday who aimed to escalate the value of what they bought. The important thing was for the graph to keep rising, whether it was toward "Mom, I'm thinking of you on your special day from far away," or toward "Forever yours." The message was in the movement, since transactions themselves were impersonal—a signature, an address in the States, the yellow duplicate of the order as receipt. But some guys would linger, browse with their gazes the shelves of display merchandise that stretched behind me. Those times we'd pretend together that they were just regular working men, thoughtful enough to have stopped off on the way home from the office to pick out a little something.

I SAW IT MORE THAN ONCE IN MY tour, the homesickness turn to fear turn to boredom turn to crazy indifference. Where a man came from got further away, where he was going got less clear. Even regulars didn't talk much to me about what went on away from the base—yet I heard enough to know not to ask for more. They left the war at my door, wiped it off on the mat I kept for mud. We shared the same color uniform, often the same year of birth, our I.D. numbers ran in a common sequence, but that's where the union ended. I was different from a desk jockey or a chaplain—the only reports I filed were in dollars and cents, and the only confessions I heard had to do with bad credit. I was ordinary as home.

I was lonely, too, but I was safe, so I kept my mouth

shut, kept to myself, maybe out of embarrassment, maybe out of how easy a target I could become. I didn't even hang around with the other clerks, it was that bad. Sometime after my first quarterly report, I switched from two letters home a month to one, and mostly wrote about the hot weather, implying I was forbidden to reveal my exact whereabouts or the particulars of my daily activities. Probably I let myself get fixed too hard on my special clients, the ones I thought about and waited for. Of all of them, Joe Peck and Bob Diggs were at the top of my list, from that first day they came in together.

Joe was the one you had to notice because he never shut up. He'd ask me, upon entering, what were the specials of the day? He had a way of winking when he talked, as though he was letting you in on an idea nobody but you and he understood. Nothing brought him down.

"Going out of business," I answered when he tried the line the first time. "Prices slashed. Chance of a lifetime."

"Stereos two for one? A fine gold chain with every purchase over one hundred dollars?"

"Green stamps," I said. "Sign up now for our tropical vacation holiday."

Joe stopped, looked me over. Up to then I had been pure woodwork, an excuse for the sound of his voice.

"We got us a live wire," he joked to his buddy. "A regular Bob Hope, here to entertain the troops."

"Ann-Margret's in the back, changing her dress," I said. "Next show in twenty minutes."

"I'm a Martha Raye man, myself." Joe introduced Diggs, who barely nodded.

"Where you guys from?"

"Ohio," Joe said.

"I hear the Buckeyes are running low on cultured Japanese pearls. A sad fact on Mother's Day. Luckily I have a few strings in stock, direct from the oyster ranches of Yokohama."

"Pearls," he considered. I didn't have to quote the price.

"Eighteen- or twenty-inch strand?"

"Twenty. One for every year."

"A wise choice," I agreed, and wrote up the order. Diggs, the other guy, didn't buy a thing. Tight, I decided.

The second time I saw Joe I was crossing the yard on the way to the barracks and he was with his company, getting ready to head out. Without thinking, I waved and was relieved when he saluted back.

"See you next week," he called as he piled into a jeep next to Diggs.

"Washington's Birthday in July." I spread my arms wide.

Joe elbowed Diggs. "Crazy Eddie." He pointed at me. "The bargain hunter's best friend."

That's how I came by my nickname. When the two of them showed up at the store ten days later, Joe's left arm wrapped in an Ace and splint, his dark face was tired, his lips cracked. I produced no discount but recommended a new Bulova to replace the one that had shattered.

"What do I get for fifty-nine ninety-five?" he wanted to know.

I read the description. "Self-winding, water resistant, shockproof, ten-year guarantee."

"Starting now." Joe signed the chit and pushed it toward me. "Ten years of perfect time or you'll hear from my lawyer."

"Crazy Eddie stands behind his word," I said and raised my right palm.

"A wild man." Joe shook his head, used the counter to fold his receipt one-handed into his brown wallet. Diggs wasn't wounded but he seemed nervous, on the run. He left with Joe, then returned alone almost immediately, got me to himself.

"You do layaway here?" he wanted to know. "Long-term?"

I slid the green account book forward. "Fill in your name, serial number, item desired, and amount to be automatically docked from your wages," I instructed. "Then don't give it another thought."

Diggs turned the pages of my catalog slowly, waiting for inspiration. He'd keep a place with his finger, then surrender it for somewhere else. Finally he made his selection, pushed the book back to me. I looked where he pointed—the one-carat diamond solitaire set in platinum. At the price quoted, I didn't get many takers, so my interest was up.

"That ring is top of the line. A one-of-a-kind keepsake. Someone pretty special back home?"

Diggs's face was grim and didn't reveal a thing.

"Sure. Dozens." He slammed the binder. "It's the most expensive thing you sell, right?"

"Absolutely. Primo." I watched him enter the amount he wanted deducted—almost half his wages every check. "Even at that rate it'll be nearly a year," I warned him.

"You'll mark it every time? I can come by and see, like in a passbook?"

"First National," I said. "U.S.-government insured."

And Diggs did show, two or three times the first weeks and regular after that, but always when he was by himself. He opened the ledger to his page, stared at the growing column of figures that marched toward the diamond. And over those months he changed. By the halfway mark Diggs had become one of those who grin too much, who mumble to themselves. He wore a charm around his neck, something Joe bragged that Diggs had "found" in the jungle. After the first glance I didn't inspect it closely. He never bought anything else, just stashed his earnings, built equity. When the ring was two-thirds paid he varied his routine and asked a question.

"What would happen now, if—you know—I failed to make the final installments?"

I was just back from my R & R at Waikiki. I had stayed at a big hotel with a balcony facing the beach. Every time I looked at the water I heard the theme music from "Hawaii Five-0" in my head, and it had made me homesick. I didn't want to bear bad news, but I had no choice but to give Diggs the regulation answer.

"The money you've paid would be returned to your account," I explained. "But no interest. That's the downside of layaway."

"And the ring?"

I shook my head, wanting to apologize for the heartlessness of bookkeeping. I expected Diggs to be pissed, to demand that the ring go anyway to whatever girl he intended it for, but instead he flashed that private smile, went deep into himself for a second before he spoke.

"I'll make you a deal, Eddie," he said, calling me that name for the first time. "Keep the goddamn money. I miss one time, it's your pot."

Joe Peck happened to be in the store that day, scoping out a set of audio components shipped in a single unit to wherever they were sent: turntable on top, receiver on the bottom, eight-track deck sandwiched between. It was listed at $499 and he had offered $350, then $400, and was up to $450-not-a-penny-more. He couldn't believe what he was hearing from Diggs.

"Keep the money? Keep the fucking money? Man, you've been in the jungle too long. How about I stake you, buy into the deal? Take over the payments if you miss a couple? You can owe me." Joe turned to me. "That ring's all he lives for. He don't want to lose it."

But Diggs was already out the door, still laughing at the joke.

WHEN THE BIG DAY OF THE FINAL installment arrived, I was prepared—had the actual diamond there in a jeweler's box, though ordinarily I never kept valuable items in active inventory. Diggs showed up right on schedule to check the debit and I set the ring on the counter beneath the hooded bulb. It rested on crushed blue velvet, a hundred facets reflecting dark light.

A full house was assembled for the occasion—guys who served with Diggs who'd heard about his layaway so often that it seemed a part of their own tours. Joe leaned against the doorjamb, crowded in with lots of others. I felt something myself—pride at completing a sale so costly, of an item that would appreciate. Relief, too, that it had all worked out without a hitch. Maybe even a little sad that the game was finally over.

Diggs picked up the ring, examined it from every angle. Then he put it back, shook his head.

"Changed my mind," he said, low but loud enough. "Can the last deduction. This time I'll go for the Rolex." He opened my green book to the page he knew by heart and pointed to the next blank line.

There was a pause, a silence like the smooth band that separates the cuts between two songs on an album. I didn't get it, not for a minute. I was disappointed, you might say my reputation was insulted and at stake. Every eye in the room was on the ring, as though that rock was some crystal ball, as though it had a mysterious life of its own.

I broke the spell. I told Diggs I was prepared to reapply his accumulated total—which was more than plenty to pay for the watch. I told him he had his choice of anything in my catalog, just say the word.

But Joe Peck must have remembered what Diggs

had told me about a missed payment, must have thought I'd be low enough to take Diggs up on that offer, and he cut me off.

"How much, man? What's the final hit?"

"No way," I interrupted. "My call." I reached into the register and counted out the amount needed from his next paycheck. "The ring's yours," I said to Diggs. "Special G.I. Bill discount. Crazy Eddie will not be undersold."

The thing was, there were no whistles, no hoots of approval. No one even applauded. The guys took their cue from Diggs, who was staring at me, his face drained and white, trying for his grin and not finding it.

"I'm serious," I said. "You bought it."

I took the ring from the box, lobbed it to Diggs, but when he made no move to reach out, it struck his chest, fell to the floor. You could hear it hit the plywood, the room was that quiet.

"Fuck you, man. Just fuck you." Diggs backed away, turned, shoved a path through the standing men. You could hear the rain through the door he left open, hear it pound and blow without cooling the air.

The grunts shuffled out, pulling the hoods of their ponchos over their heads and ducking their faces, careful of the ring where it lay. Finally only Joe was left.

"Take it," I said. "He'll change his mind. Talk to him. Tell him there's no obligation."

Joe looked at me, not in anger, I'm sure of that, just kind of hard and steady. I thought he was about to say something, but instead he gave a low whistle, then left.

There's a hollowness you feel the minute after a full room empties. You're aware of other possibilities, of something missing. The space seems like the inside of a bell. I opened the gate and walked across to the diamond. The sound of my footsteps was heavy and dry, each one as crisp as the turn of a page.

AFTER DIGGS DISAPPEARED, MY business turned to poison. Soldiers still bought, but from the other clerks, timed their visits to the PX for when I was off-duty. Even Joe Peck let anniversaries pass.

"How's things doing in Ohio?" I asked him one day in the mess hall, and he just answered, "Hanging loose."

Since Diggs was officially MIA, his wages kept coming through, and every second Friday I entered an installment into the ledger against his watch. In my last two months on that job, he was my solitary customer.

Then my supervisor noticed, canceled the order, and paid back his account.

I NEVER SAW THE ENEMY FACE TO face, never heard his voice. I never fired a shot in anger or in self-defense. I never got my face on the TV news or my name in *Stars and Stripes* or carved into a granite wall. I never went AWOL, never smoked dope but twice, never had a date with a bar girl.

But I like to think I lightened a few loads, helped give pleasure to the friends and relations of my customers, honestly recommended quality when asked to do so. I opened on time and stayed late if there was a line waiting. I've got not a damn thing to be ashamed of.

But I don't have much to contribute when other vets start telling their glory tales. At the Ridgeway Post VFW, where I'm a member with my dad, I drink a beer and listen as they go around the table—an ambush competing with an asshole sergeant, a stint as a POW versus a Purple Heart for valor. On late nights when they've all had their say, when they don't want to go home and they signal for a last round, it comes my turn. I dig the chain with the ring on it from under my shirt, drop it in a clean ashtray, let them wonder. The stone still quiets a room with its gleam.

SHINING AGATE

The Journal of Comparative Ethnography,
vol. 31, no. 6 (Summer 1989):118–126.

*T*HERE WAS A BEAUTIFUL YOUNG WOMAN *named Shining Agate, the oldest of three daughters, and she was very proud. Always, she insisted that her hair flow loose and free of tangles, that her dress be sewn from the most supple skins, that the meat of her soup be tender and cut into very small pieces. To her parents' eyes, Shining Agate could do no wrong, even in the smallest thing, and they never welcomed into their longhouse anyone who suggested otherwise. As a result, Shining Agate grew up convinced of her own perfection, a conviction so powerful and sure that by* the time she was twenty almost everyone in the village agreed with her.

Whatever special place Shining Agate preferred immediately became the most desirable spot to visit. Whatever flower made Shining Agate smile became the favorite blossom of every woman, old or still a child. Whatever song, whatever tale, whatever color of the sky pleased Shining Agate, that song or tale or color became for a time the delight of the world.

Now it happened that there was a young man named Left Hand, who was the oldest of two brothers—his younger brother was named Right Hand. For as long as he could remember, Left Hand had dreamed that someday Shining Agate would consent to be his wife, but he was afraid to ask because of course he did not feel worthy of her. Certainly he was a good hunter, an excellent trapper, a weaver of tight, impenetrable fishnets. Certainly he was strong and robust. Certainly the mothers of many young women had invited him to sample the foods their daughters prepared, but none of those daughters interested him. Shining Agate was the only wife Left Hand desired.

"What can I do?" he asked Right Hand. "How can I make her accept me?"

Right Hand was a devoted brother and wanted to help, but to him Shining Agate was too proud, too happy with herself. To him, her beauty was not that great, her ideas not that amusing, her smiles not that charming. It was as though Right Hand saw Shining Agate through a mist that obscured

231

her brightness, and because of that, he judged her more clearly than anyone else. He did not find her a bad young woman, but he did consider her vain. Most of all, he hated for his brother to be so unhappy at Shining Agate's expense.

"She is a woman the same as any other, just as you are a man the same as any other," Right Hand told Left Hand. "Perhaps she will accept you, perhaps not. You will never know unless you inquire."

Left Hand trusted Right Hand and listened to his advice. The next day when he encountered Shining Agate playing stick games with her sisters, he took a breath and spoke to her.

"I have it in mind to marry," he said softly. "Do you think I can find a wife for myself?"

Shining Agate looked up and noticed Left Hand as she never had before. He was tall and the sun danced on the blackness of his hair. His voice was frightened, his eyes bright, his skin without flaw. For some time she had wondered why no man had yet mentioned marriage to her when even women much younger had found husbands, and she felt a surge of gratitude toward Left Hand for removing this worry from her heart. She smiled on his question, and answered with the words he had hoped to hear.

"Of course," she said without laughter, surprising her sisters. "You must only ask permission of the mother of the wife you prefer and I'm sure she will agree."

No sooner had the news passed through the village—for Shining Agate's sisters were anxious to tell, glad to think of

Shining Agate as married and out of their way—than people decided that Left Hand was truly an exceptional young man, even better than they had previously realized. Everyone was glad to celebrate the union, and was certain that it would produce many healthy children. No one was ever happier than Left Hand.

Yet soon after the marriage, Shining Agate experienced a curious change. Now that she found herself with a husband who approved of her every action, who complimented her sixteen times each day, who insisted upon repeating her every observation to anyone who would listen, and who felt so shy in her presence that he dared not touch her or ask anything of her without some prior signal that she welcomed the request, Shining Agate, for the first time in her life, became tired of praise.

Only occasionally at first, but ever more frequently, she intentionally tested her husband's devotion. Some days she would not comb her hair with the hawk's claw that made it smooth, but even then Left Hand would look at her and sigh: "How beautiful you are, Shining Agate. What a sunrise for my eyes." Some nights as they lay together beneath their fur covers she would wait until Left Hand was nearly asleep and then poke him sharply with her elbow or kick him with the heel of her foot. He would wake instantly, but instead of asking her to be still, he would say, his voice low and whispering, "How wonderful to be reminded that you are by my side." Some days Shining Agate would boil the stew meat with salmonberry leaves, making it bitter and sour, but Left

Hand would only flatter the taste. Some nights Shining Agate would push Left Hand away when he rolled against her in passion, but he would shut his eyes peacefully and dream of her instead.

"I would do anything for you," Left Hand promised Shining Agate every morning. "No task is too large."

Finally Shining Agate could endure her husband no longer.

"I have heard there is a pure white wolverine deep in the forest," she told Left Hand. "Go seek it for me and don't return until you can bring me the skin for a hat."

Left Hand looked out the doorway. It was early winter and the snows were already heavy upon the ground.

"Surely such an animal will already be asleep deep in its den," he replied. "In the springtime I will trap it and make the hat for you myself."

"Wolverines don't sleep in the winter like bears," Shining Agate reminded him. "And I won't need a hat in the spring-time. Go now. Find the pure white wolverine and don't return without it. Was your promise a lie?"

Left Hand gathered up his bow, his snowshoes, and his parka. "It was the truth," he assured Shining Agate as he left the longhouse.

What Left Hand did not know was that Shining Agate had made up the story of the pure white wolverine. No such animal had ever been seen.

Days passed, then weeks, then months, and still Left

Hand did not come back to the village. At first Shining Agate was relieved. She visited with her sisters, slept on her back, and ate whatever and whenever she pleased from the ample provisions Left Hand had stored for the winter. Sometimes she did not think even once of her husband between sunrise and sundown, between sundown and sunrise, and tried to convince herself that she was again exactly as she had been before her marriage.

But certain things could not be changed back. When women of the village remarked to her that no wife had ever been so brave at the prospect of a lost husband, Shining Agate could not enjoy their words. When young men began to leave fine pelts and fresh moose meat by her door, she could not receive their gifts as her due. When her parents offered her comfort and sympathy, she could not bear their kindness.

Instead, she sought out the company of the only person who frowned whenever he beheld her, for Right Hand would not forgive Shining Agate his brother's disappearance.

"Sister-in-law," he said one morning as they stood together at the hole in the ice from which lake water was drawn. "Is your head cold today? Would the fur of a white wolverine keep you warmer?"

Shining Agate saw herself through Right Hand's eyes— selfish, cruel, and greedy—and it was as though a heavy cloak had fallen from her shoulders and her arms were free to move.

*"No condemnation you can say is bad enough for me,"
she told Right Hand. The joy in her voice surprised him so*

thoroughly that he put down his oiled basket and stared at her face.

"Sister-in-law," he tried again. "Have you not been sleeping well? Your face is gray and older than I remember."

"I do not deserve sleep," Shining Agate replied. "I do not deserve to be called 'Sister' by the brother of my husband."

"I am too harsh with you," Right Hand apologized. "My brother will be angry when he returns."

"He will not return," Shining Agate said. "You are not harsh enough." And with that she plunged her arm into the icy water, her face bright in pain.

"Shining Agate, stop this," Right Hand cried, and pulled her up. He tucked her dripping arm inside his parka, hugged it against his chest to keep it warm. This touch was lightning in a summer sky, and soon it happened that every night Right Hand slept in his brother's house, and Shining Agate never turned away from his embrace.

Even then the people of the village found nothing to criticize. "How appropriate," they agreed. "The grieving widow is consoled by the loyal brother-in-law who fulfills his obligation." But Shining Agate paid no attention, and one late night, after Right Hand was too in love with her to hate her, she told him the truth about the pure white wolverine and why he need not worry that Left Hand would come home.

A year passed, another, a further spring. Shining Agate bore a handsome son whom she named Laughter, and who, like his father, reached only with his right hand. In the summer they moved to a fish camp down the inlet and, guarded by their secrets, the lovers made each day different and better than the one before. Laughter justified his name, and the cabin was filled with his merriment.

On the first day of the last summer moon, however, a rumor flashed through the village: Left Hand was on his way.

"How did he survive?" people asked when they heard the news.

"He almost froze," they were told. "He broke his leg in a fall and had made his death song when he heard wide-spaced footsteps. It was the Sesquatch, bear people who lived in the world before human beings and who now live only in the highest mountains. They took pity on Left Hand and carried him back to their village. They used their ancient magic to set the bone of his leg, but it was a bad break and took many months to heal. Even by the first summer, Left Hand was still too weak to return and so he stayed with the Sesquatch another year, hunted with them, became wise in their ways. When his full strength at last returned, he taught them human skills in gratitude for their hospitality, but their fingers were too blunt to tie sinew dense enough to catch salmon, so Left Hand stayed through the spring and early summer and left behind forty-eight nets of his own construction. The Sesquatch gave him as a sign of their friendship and appreciation a prize of great rarity: the pelt of a pure white wolverine.

When Right Hand heard of his brother's adventures his face turned to stone. Without speaking, he ran from the fish *camp. Shining Agate grabbed up Laughter and rushed after him, but by the time she reached the beach, Right Hand had already pushed out his boat and was digging his paddle into the sea, heading toward the sun.*

"Take me, take me," Shining Agate called, and waded far into the foaming surf. She held Laughter high above her head, but in his shame Right Hand would not look back. "You can't deny me. I will be too lonely," Shining Agate cried, and stumbled further and further from shore. The water passed her knees, passed her waist, and finally it passed her shoulders until only her head and her arms, holding high her smiling son, were visible.

When it became clear to Shining Agate that Right Hand would not come back, that she must face Left Hand without him, her heart turned cold and smooth. She lowered her strong arms, sank Laughter deep beneath the waves, hugged him against her chest until he stopped moving. Then her own legs were caught by the undertow, and she disappeared. The surface of the ocean was once again empty and calm.

—As collected from Sergei Mishikoff,
Suscitna, Alaska,
August 1970

"Sir," the annoyed flight attendant addressed me. "This airplane cannot move unless everyone is seated."

Everyone was me, and I wasn't, and yet we were. I

pleasantly pointed out this paradox to illustrate the capriciousness of codified law: what shouldn't be, nevertheless was.

She was not intrigued. "Sit," she ordered curtly, and, faced with a direct command, I obeyed.

I was on my way to Alaska, propelled by inertia. Three years ago I had enrolled in a graduate anthropology program and, having taken the required course work for six semesters, it only remained for me to prove myself in the field. I had no ambitious queries of my own to resolve, so I appropriated one from my adviser, Abraham Wentworth. While passing through a remote subarctic village in 1927, a question arose in his mind that he had never answered to his own satisfaction: Why did human beings remain in this remote, cold, barren environment?

"Find out," he directed me. "It'll be good for at least a major publication or two."

So here I was, my stowed bags packed with painkillers and antiseptics, my sensitive film protected against weather by tied condoms, my future as a respected professional in the balance, aboard a flight diagonal across the continent. My fellow passengers were Japanese businessmen on their way home to Tokyo, healthy hikers, mothers grim-lipped from saying good-bye to their daughters-in-law and knowing, despite protests and promises, that their own solicitous faces would fade within a day from the memory of their drawling grandchildren.

It was one of those endless journeys in which all sense of from and to is lost, when secrets are confided to seatmates, great thoughts are pondered but not written down, plans are made that will never be carried out. It was a two-meal, two-hot-towel flight, a dislocating hang in the air, and by the time I arrived I'd be a time traveler: no longer truly from where I'd started but not yet one with where I'd come.

O NCE IN SUSCITNA, I WAS GIVEN over to the care of small children until I was educated enough to deal with adults without taxing their patience. It took months for me to learn the rudiments of the language—the local dialect varied widely from anything previously published—and so I spent my first days shepherded by reluctant young boys or girls to whom parents had assigned the chore of my improvement. Aimlessly I followed one or another of them along the lanes of the community, pointing at objects and dutifully repeating the name to my instructor's satisfaction before phonetically transcribing it into my notebook.

I had arrived in the early autumn, naively treating my stint of fieldwork as if it conformed to a standard academic calendar. Within weeks the sun all but disappeared from the murky sky, the temperature fell permanently below zero, and my child-hosts returned to their classrooms for hours each day. Time dragged, its waste insufferable whenever I imagined the activities I could engage in elsewhere, the conversations I could carry on, the tasks I could accomplish. Winter was a long, insomniac night, featureless and infuriating, in which events occurred only to vaguely blur together in their recollection. My vocabulary lists lengthened, my hair grew, my connections to the world outside the village frayed and snapped.

One day in March, warmer than most, unable to endure the indoor boredom, I ventured out alone on a path bound high on either side by hard-packed snow. Turning a sharp corner, I saw in the gloom a deeper shadow, tall and menacing. A bear—it must be—hungry from hibernation, out, like me, for the first time. Running was pointless, so I did a thing I'd read about: I dropped to the ground, shut my eyes, and lay completely still. A bear was supposed to believe me dead and therefore unappetizing or unthreatening, anything, to convince it to avoid me. My ears strained for the scrape of paws, the low rumble of a growl. Was it staring at me, transfixed in wonder? Finally I opened one eye and found myself alone, the only spot of color in a vast whiteness.

My immediate terror broadened. I dreaded loneliness, failure, accident. I saw myself drifting within a
pointless life, defined by cautious habit, oscillating
along the short curve between amusement and annoyance. It was as incorrect to say that nothing mattered to
me as it was to claim that something did. At last the
cold penetrated my goosedown parka. I stood up, re-
traced my steps, went back inside. Two o'clock. In an
hour school would end and perhaps a child would be
sent to visit.

I HAD BEEN RESIDENT IN SUSCITNA
for eight months before I felt reasonably fluent. Even
then, I had no choice but to frequently interrupt my
eavesdropping with requests for repetitions, explanations, distinct pronunciations. I fit into no preestab-
lished category within the existing social structure of
the village, and so uniquely came to fill my own niche,
a role approximately described as "nosy, inept, non-
contributory stranger." In the eyes of my informants it
must have seemed as though I fairly panted for any
scrap of simply expressed gossip, historical or modern,
and a few of them took delight in leading me astray,
exhorting me to speak inappropriate words. I had no
alternative but to become the butt of bad jokes, an
irresistible buffoon, a moron who could be counted

upon to laugh with the crowd at his own stupidities. How else to ingratiate myself? Anger or resentment would have resulted only in an attitude toward me of indifference or scorn, and the thrust of my work depended upon access. And so I hid my true feelings, reserved my sarcasm and wit for letters that would be appreciatively read thousands of miles to the south, and bided my time. When this exile was over, my voice would be restored.

In the interim, there was the place. Denied the distraction of conversation, I had no choice but to interact with my surroundings, to open myself to their feel and sound, to the salt in the unflagging wind. After the months of darkness, the return of daylight was exhilarating, thrilling. The air smelled brown and green, the sky abounded with calling birds, the ice retreated each day further from the shore, and beneath its transparent glare could be seen flashes of movement as insects skated the widening pockets. Roads turned to mud, mud to caked ruts. Men heated rocks for sweatbaths and children forgot their coats when they went out to play. At Easter a man, Ivan Kroto, went to church drunk. He sat and knelt and prayed loudly out of rhythm with the rest of the congregation, and no one minded. His behavior made them smile.

That summer, I moved from the village to an abandoned fish camp, where I lived alone in a tar paper–

covered shanty perched high on a bluff, its one glass window fronting the blue-gray of Cook Inlet. From that solitary eye, one July dawn, I spied movement on the rocky beach and quickly descended the steps—planks pushed into the crumbling slope—to find a seal pup the tide had left stranded. It stared up at me, trusting and curious, too surprised at the firmness of land to propel itself back to water, and allowed me to stroke its sleek fur. I kept it safe, protected from the sun by a crate, through the slow revolution of the sea's cycle, and the next day it was gone.

I filled those hours I allotted to myself with projects and assignments. Each night I would transcribe the notes I had collected, bits of new village trivia, emendations to previously recorded data, chance insights, lines of inquiry to pursue in future. Most mornings when the tide was out I walked the beach, my eyes screening the pebbles for good luck. Among the dozens of locally identified charms, none was more prized than an opaque, soft, orange stone, slightly translucent when held before a light. Encased within, like the grain of sand around which in warmer oceans a pearl is formed, was a dark core of rock, and the smaller the heart, the greater the potency. I kept a collection in a mayonnaise jar on my table.

In winter I had eaten the charity of others—donated moose meat, muskrat, dried fish. But in the summer, I caught my own salmon with a nylon net I stretched between two barrels and anchored thirty feet offshore. First came the humpies, then kings, and reds, as run followed run. I supplemented my diet with boiled noodles, instant potatoes, Rice-A-Roni, or Hamburger Helper in a rotation of the six flavors stocked by the village all-purpose store. I drank tea, instant coffee, or Kool-Aid, watched the skies for the mail plane. Each night I listened to country music on KYAK, or to the cassette tapes I had culled from my collection at home and brought north to keep me company. For society, I lost copiously but with forced grace at pinochle or cribbage, the village's twin obsessions. For work, I amassed indiscriminate information from anyone I could persuade to talk to me.

P ARTICIPANT-OBSERVATION IS THE name of the game in cultural anthropology, and accordingly I had apprenticed myself to Nikefor Alexan, the experienced fisherman whose one-room summer fish camp lay six miles from the village. With plywood, borrowed tools, a door and a window ordered from Anchorage, I constructed a makeshift cabin on a flat clearing a mile up the beach.

Nikefor, his wife Madrona, their infant daughter Mary, and Madrona's father Sergei Mishikoff were a quiet family, traditionals who spoke no English and practiced a religion that combined old beliefs with the more recent teachings of nineteenth-century Russian Orthodox missionaries.

I was under no illusion that I was much help to Nikefor with fishing—an extra pair of arms, albeit clumsy and needing constant instruction—but for the group as a whole I believe I provided mild diversion. Though they rarely asked me questions about my background, they suffered my own queries with patience and good humor. In the evenings, during the preparations for supper, the mending of the nets, the sorting of the hooks, I was their excuse to repeat old stories and jokes, a fresh audience who never failed to signify interest and enthusiasm. My tape recorder was always available.

We were not friends, these people and I—too much divided us—but we grew used to each other's presence, began to relax our respective guards. They knew by and large what to expect from me, and I had gauged, more or less, when to laugh. We shared food and labor, weather and isolation, and within the parentheses of the warmer season, we constituted a kind of unit. I felt myself part of a process I had read about in fieldwork courses: the researcher's perspective shifts over the course of his investigation from that of a complete outsider to something approximating an insider's point of view. Oddness is replaced by ordinary, novelty by routine. I had experienced the loneliness I had so dreaded in anticipating my stay in Suscitna, but over time the emotion had evolved and altered. Solitude became my most cherished companion, my trusted friend. After a long day of my own fawning, exhausting smiles, I sought it out.

SILVERS ARE THE LAST SALMON TO return from the open sea to seek for spawning the streams where they were hatched, and this season, as July turned into August, their appearance was behind schedule. The preference of the canneries, which were our prime source of cash income, an abundance of silvers was directly proportional to the village's prosperity, and so we watched for them impatiently.

"They're smart," Nikefor commented. He sat in shirtsleeves at the table, a hand of solitaire dealt before him. He wore his dark hair long, combed to a ducktail in the back. "They'll come at night when they think we're asleep, or during a storm when they believe we won't take out the boat."

Not sure whether to nod or smile, I lifted Mary from her playpen and rocked her in my arms.

Madrona stood stirring an iron pot on the wood-stove. When the water reached a high boil she spooned in chunks of fresh fish, a can of green beans, a can of beets.

"Watch for a light," Nikefor addressed me. "If the silvers come when I can't send for you overland, I'll put the lantern on the boat. You come down from your camp and I'll pick you up."

The logistics of my living arrangement were a frequent source of worry for Nikefor. At high tide the beach between our two camps was swamped under four feet of water, and the danger from bears was too great to permit passage along the top of the bluffs at night. He wanted me to sleep on his floor to insure my availability the moment the run started. Every day he tried to persuade me, but I refused to surrender my few hours of privacy.

"Stay here tonight, why don't you?" he offered. "Look, the tide is already up to your ankles. You'll get wet if you leave now."

"I have my hip boots," I reminded him. "I'll watch for your light."

"You should listen," Madrona said. She reached her hand into a huge bag of dried potato flakes, came up with a fistful, and then dramatically tossed these into her stew. This technique was her specialty, a conjurer's trick that both thickened the broth and created a skim of tiny dumplings. "This time of year those ghosts you are always asking about will come and get you if they find you walking alone at night."

I looked over Mary's head at Sergei, who made his eyes round in mock fright. My preoccupation with collecting ghost stories was a cause of much teasing. Grown men and women, it was implied, had more important things to think about.

THE WAVES KNOCKED AT MY KNEES as I sloshed toward my cabin. The night was moonless, overcast, with a promise of autumn in the chill air. I judged distance by the one constant marker located halfway along my route, a stagnant tidal pool that always stank of rotting seaweed. Once I passed by it, my stairs were only fifteen minutes further ahead. By the time I climbed them and closed my door, the Inlet had reached nearly four feet up the cliffs. I could imagine Nikefor squinting into the night, frustrated and suspicious, wondering if the silvers would take this murky opportunity to evade his nets. I switched on my battery lamp, dropped a Roberta Flack tape into the player, and finished the day's notes: *N. bullshitting me about believing fish can think? S.'s reaction suggests yes. M. warns me about bogeyman as she would a kid. Cross-check child abduction tales. Function: To keep people inside at night? To instill group dependence?*

Roberta sang "Do What You Gotta Do." I clicked off my lamp, lay on my cot, and zipped myself into my sleeping bag. Four months to go, minimum, before I left this place. I yawned deeply and turned onto my side. A few minutes later the machine automatically shut itself off and I let myself be lulled by the regular rhythm of the surf, approaching, approaching, approaching.

Suddenly I was alert, listening to light footsteps ascend the planks, reach the narrow porch. I waited for a voice, a knock, but . . . nothing. An animal, I decided once I thought about it. No one could have crossed the beach after me because of the deepening water. I must have been dreaming.

I recomposed myself, opened a gate for my mind to wander.

There it was again: footfalls, definitely. And there, I smelled the sour odor from down the shore, so it must be Nikefor or Sergei, come to tell me the salmon were making a dash for safe passage. I heard a tap against the wooden door.

"Tinashdit-ah," I spoke in Suscitna.

Another tap, soft as a branch moved by an evening breeze.

"Tinashdit, come in."

No answer, but wait, I caught the unmistakable sound of stifled giggling. This was a joke, a follow-up to Madrona's imprecation about ghosts. Scare the *bergunidge,* the outsider, with his own research.

"Aikda," I called. "I'm already in bed. Pull out the latch string and come in before you fall into the water."

A silence . . . then a loud rapping—bang-bang-bang-bang—but still no words.

"Please yourself," I said. "But I'm not getting up in the cold to play along."

And all was still, utterly still. No retreating steps, no protests, no whispers. Through the four panes of my window glass, the stars were steady and familiar, balanced in their distant silence. I made a mental note to find out how Nikefor got from his camp to mine and, more importantly, to ascertain his motive. I hadn't realized that my reactions mattered enough that he would risk getting wet to provoke them.

THE TIDE WAS SUFFICIENTLY OUT BY five A.M. and soon thereafter I sat in my place at the Alexan table, ready for breakfast. Alaska Fish and Wildlife restricted fishing in the Inlet to the hours between seven and four during silver season, and enforced the ruling by sending officers in small planes to overfly the beach in unpredictable patterns.

"*Ya l'ida,* how did you sleep?" Madrona asked me.

"*Ya li aleh,* okay, once I was left alone." I gave Nikefor a meaningful look.

"Left alone?" Madrona was a good actress: her expression seemed genuinely puzzled.

"Ask your husband."

Nikefor had been listening to the radio for the weather report, and glanced up.

"What I want to know," I said, "is how you got from here to my place once the tide came in. How you got back home again. It's a good trick."

"What are you talking about?"

"I knew you'd say that."

I turned to Sergei, expecting a reciprocating grin, but his face was blank.

"All right, all right, if you insist," I said, and with as much sarcasm as I could muster in a language not my own, I told my story.

Nikefor, Madrona, and Sergei had stopped what they were doing and listened closely.

"You should have come in," I finished.

No one moved, no one replied.

"Come on," Nikefor said at last, and walked out of the cabin. Madrona wrapped Mary in a blanket and followed. Sergei splashed water on the fire in the stove and beckoned me to precede him down the stairs to the shore.

"Are we going to fish now?" I asked, surprised that we had packed no lunch.

No answer. Instead, once we were all assembled below, the group began to walk the beach, past the empty boat, in the direction of Suscitna.

"What are we doing? Where are we going now?"

No answer. They were pointedly ignoring me, treating me with what anthropology textbooks termed "ritual avoidance." But why, to what purpose? After a while we went by without breaking stride the stairs up to my shanty, and a mile beyond we reached the next fish camp. Theodore Kroto and his teenage son Max had already loaded nets into their boat and were ready to push off. Wordlessly, the rest of us waited while Nikefor approached them. I couldn't hear what was said, but I saw Nikefor gesture back in the direction of our camps, registered the worry in his face. Theodore dug his boot into the sand, nodded once, twice, and finally, in what seemed like an attitude of resignation, threw the anchor from his boat. Max ran to their cabin, and in less than two minutes returned with his mother and younger brother. Quietly excited, they joined us as we resumed our march.

At each camp along the way, a similar sequence occurred. In some instances, boats already launched were summoned back to shore. Laundry was left piled half washed in rushing streams. Nothing was allowed to delay us, and no one we encountered stayed behind, so that soon we were a ragtag crowd of maybe twenty-five men and women, children, babies, and a few trailing dogs. The only noise was the drum of our feet on sand and rock, the rustle of people in a hurry.

I was confused beyond anything I had ever experienced. To my knowledge the forfeit of a fishing day was unthinkable, impossible. In Suscitna, what wasn't caught and preserved in August could not be consumed in February—there were no second chances. As I kept pace between Sergei and Madrona I considered every explanation for this trek, from sudden illness to my own abrupt eviction. Whatever was coming, I was without preparation or defense.

At last, just after noon, the straggling entourage arrived at the entrance to the tiny Russian Orthodox church in Suscitna. Father Peter Oskolov, part Native though from a different community, listened to Sergei's whispered news and disappeared into the sacristy. He emerged in a purple funerary stole, carrying a gold ciborium in one hand and an ornate metal censer in the other.

I had long since given up asking questions, so I didn't try to catch his eye as we proceeded to the next stop, a log cabin without electricity or running water, the lifelong residence of the oldest woman in Suscitna. Martina Stephan was small and frail, her spine doubled over by osteoporosis. Balding and deeply wrinkled, she was never seen without a black shawl draped over her head. Like the subject of a Goya painting, her hands were forged by arthritis, twisted into attitudes of perpetual supplication. Her voice was harsh, rattling as wind through a gravelly passage, and her eyes were clouded white with glaucoma. She could not have weighed much more than eighty pounds.

"Grandmother," Sergei shouted into her ear as we all stood watching outside the open door. "Bring your hat and come with us. We need you."

Martina gravely dropped her head even further than its natural posture, then raised it. She shuffled further into the dark interior, where she rooted among boxes and bags stacked against the far wall. When she moved back into my field of vision she clutched a small bundle wrapped inside a piece of faded olive green army blanket. Bunky George, the manager of the store, pulled up in his Jeep, and Sergei and Nikefor lifted Martina into the passenger seat. The rest of us climbed into the beds of what seemed like every pickup in the village, and in a long, jarring procession we raced the incoming tide back down the rocky beach to the steps that led to my fish camp.

I jumped to the ground, made to go first. I couldn't

remember the condition of my room: Had I put away my notes? Straightened my cot? Neatness was a value among the Suscitna and I dreaded further embarrassment.

Sergei touched my arm. "First the priest and the old lady." The fatherly, almost affectionate tone of his voice surprised me. Whatever else he was, he wasn't angry with me.

Nikefor lifted Martina in his arms, carried her like a baby, and matched Peter Oskolov, plank by plank up the side of the bluff. Madrona, Theodore, Sergei, and I came next, followed by what seemed like most of the population of Suscitna. When he reached the porch, Nikefor gently stood Martina on her feet and stepped back to watch with the rest of us while Oskolov lit his incense and Martina, with jerks and fumbles, unwrapped the blanket. I smelled mothballs as the covering fell to the ground.

The priest began to chant in Slavonic, the words indistinct and rumbling, to swing the censer in an arc. Martina reached up her arms, pulled off her shawl, and set a hat made of fur on her smooth, shining head. It was grayish, fragile-looking, its shape flattened from storage and age, but here and there the pelage bristled magnetic, as if charged with static electricity. Wearing it, Martina seemed to straighten taller.

"I return at last," she said, loud and commanding.

"I bring what you asked and now you must be content." With that, unaided, she pushed open my door and walked inside.

All around me, I felt a relaxation of tension. The world rushed back to surround us like a high wave rolls onto a dry beach: shoulders lost their hunch, mouths loosened into smiles, children whistled, babies cried, dogs barked, the long grass bent in the sea wind.

"Tonight you'll make lots of tea," Sergei whispered in my ear. "I'll explain you your story."

My work in Suscitna was different afterwards, in the six more months I remained. I had crossed a line, joined forces, been validated. People talked to me with less caution, and stopped playing tricks with vocabulary words. I was treated, I eventually decided, like a big, somewhat backward but favored child, a person who had been absent during a crucial time and needed for his understanding of things, his sophistication, to catch up to where he should be. There was no lack of joking, no forced solemnity, but unmistakably a sense of acceleration. I was in demand, told what questions I should ask, quizzed the next day after an interview to ensure that I had grasped the significance of what had been conveyed. When fishing was over and we all moved back to the village, I had visitors or invitations every night. I absorbed more than I could record, gained impressions that could not be quantified, forgot my notebook more and more often.

And in exchange, my hosts and guests sought but a single courtesy from me, repeated so often it became a refrain: to recount my visit from lonely Shining Agate and Laughter.

"She needed you to let her in," Sergei had pointed out that first night. "She required the door to be opened as her invitation. And just think, you would have seen her, her long hair dripping from the sea, her face beautiful and sad. She would have told you how her son was drowning, asked for your help, and of course you would have gone. Like many before . . . but see, you turned out to have more power than we thought."

"More power?" I asked him. "Why do you say that? All I did was stay in bed."

"Yes," he nodded, his face lit and pleased. "Think how unusual a thing that was for you. Always you are so anxious to indulge us. You jump when we call. You laugh at your own errors. You give away your possessions and ask for little in return. But last night, grandson, you were *rude!* That was your power! You are the man who didn't answer, the man who resisted Shining Agate, the man who at last released her by saying no."

DECORATION DAY

I OPEN MY EYES. THE NATIONAL anthem plays on my clock radio and an ant is crawling up the wall next to my bed. I have all the time in the world, so I wait, motionless, for it to come closer.

"Edna," Mama calls up the stairs.

Good Morning Kentuckiana informs me that Memorial Day 1964 will be hot as fire. I refuse to stir until the ant has approached near enough to be executed.

"Edna!" Mama again. "I've been up dressing chicken since four-thirty. Hurry on and raise your papa's flag before it don't matter anymore. Thebes won't come to us."

I slide my feet to the floor and sit, my knees cracking with the beginnings of the arthritis that runs in the family. I reach on the bed table for my *Daily Saints* and turn to May 27. Venerable Bede, I learn, was canonized for writing a history of England and translating the New Testament. When he dictated the last sentence in English of St. John, Bede told his secretary, "All is finished," and died.

The Thought for the Day concludes: "Whether we take Bede's *History* for chronology and the careful determination of dates; or his treatise on meter, which is really philological; or his Scriptural commentaries, and compare them with the efforts of a century or two before, or even with those of a century or two later, we can at once detect a difference."

I can hear Marcella downstairs, making as much noise as possible to speed me up. She'll be packing the car already and will comment to me, sometime before we leave, on the size of the trunk. "The new car," she still calls it almost two years after she closed the deal with the remains of Earl's insurance. *Her* new car, the only thing of value she owns after forty-three years of living, but I'm the one who has to drive it to the cemetery picnic today. Earl would never teach her.

"And anyhow, you drive like a man, Edna," is her

justification. "I feel safe with you behind the wheel." Marcella has begun to see herself as a cautious widow.

"Edna!" Mama's patience is expired. She's halfway up the stairs waiting for me.

The ant crosses a bunch of blue roses on the wallpaper. I crush it between my thumb and forefinger, drop it into the wastepaper basket as I go into the hall.

"Now come *on*, honey," Mama says. "You're the only one of us big enough to handle that flag. I told Dora we'd stop by before eleven and it's half past eight now. We want to beat the crowd."

The air smells gold from the chicken frying in the kitchen, and the dining room table has begun to accumulate provisions for the trunk. The fringe-bordered flag, already hooked on its gilt-topped pole, is propped ready by the front door. Against the wall beneath it is the last kitten, infected with the same distemper that has caused the rest of the litter to first grow listless and loose-boweled, then limp and shallow-breathing before death.

I stoop to pick it up in the palm of my hand, and as I rise its head lolls back. There's a light froth around its mouth.

"Edna, are you seeing to that cat?"

"I've got it, Mama." I'm the one who goes out to a job, who can ride the streetcar at night, who types, who has the library card registered in her name. Mama and Marcella are of too gentle a constitution to kill with their bare hands.

The kitten is frail, soft-boned, defined of pure suffering. It would be a crime to make it endure an hour longer.

In the closet I find a plastic sack from the cleaners, still on its hanger, and pull off the end. I make a bag of it and slip it over the kitten's head, pulling it tight around the nose and mouth, flattening out the ears. I stand in the closet doorway, looking into the cool, dim interior, smelling mothballs.

At first the kitten does not react, and then it makes a motion like a shrug. Through the clear plastic I can see it stretch open its mouth. It arches its back, tightens its muscles. It pushes stiffly against my hands, which heat and moisten its body.

"Just let it go," I whisper, my teeth set.

The kitten won't stop struggling and kicking and twisting in mindless instinct, ambitious for escape. It takes forever, but finally there are only rippling spasms, then nothing. I unwrap the plastic and the kitten's face is set in a wide-jawed grin. The opened eyes are dull, the expression is rage.

Dizzy and sick, I grope in the bottom of the closet for a shoe box, dump Marcella's new toeless pumps onto the floor, put the kitten inside, and close the lid.

The box is heavy as lead. Carefully, I hold it level under my arm so the body won't slide to one end.

"Edna, we're going to meet ourselves coming back if you don't hurry! Did you see your papa's flag?"

"I just strangled the cat," I call back, but lean the flagpole over my shoulder as I go outside, and slip it one-handed into the holder permanently screwed into the gray front-porch column. The stars and stripes hang slack in the airless morning, lifeless as when they draped Papa's casket, certifying him an honorably discharged veteran of the Spanish-American War.

The sounds coming from passing cars have a hollow clear ring that foretells a hot day. The grass is scratchy against my bare feet, and the ground looks too dried out to dig, so I tilt open the lid of the garbage can and dump the shoe box.

Marcella pauses on her way from the porch to the car. She's only two inches shorter than I am, but in the minds of everyone she's small and I'm big. She has given herself a new set for the day and her hair curls in precise bangs arranged to conceal her forehead, which she judges as too high. She has her nails done professionally. Today they are painted what we used to call "movie star red."

"You must have been up with the birds, Marcella," I say.

"Mama needed me to help her get things ready.

She's got Papa on her mind. I know. It's a sad holiday for me too since Earl."

She waits for my sympathy, but I decline to nod.

"You're just no good in the morning, Edna," she says finally. "I can't dream how you manage at that office."

She turns away from my look. We don't criticize each other out loud or directly and she has crossed the line.

"You know," she says, nervous for my reaction, "the trunk on this car is so roomy. We've got space to burn."

"Yes," I agree. "If only the aqua color had stayed true." And go into the house.

"Is that you, Edna?" Mama is in the kitchen. "Did you cut some of my roses to take?"

"I'll do it before we leave." I head for the bathroom, hook the door.

"I laid out that yellow sleeveless for you." Mama's voice has taken on a long-suffering tone. "I had to press out the wrinkles. I wish you'd learn to hang up your nice things when you're done with them."

There will be no arguing, the ironing has seen to that. Sometime during the week she'd searched for that damn dress till she found it stuffed into the bottom of a shopping bag in the back of my closet. When I wear it people say things like "Doesn't that Edna have the longest arms?" It's too tight across my hips, the wrong color for me. But Mama picked it out on sale four years ago and declared it springlike. She'd die if I threw it out. I take two aspirin to clear my head.

By the time I emerge, the dining room table is full: lemons and sugar, a big bowl of potato salad, napkins, a coconut cake, twin vases, and a jug for carrying water from the well on the edge of the graveyard. Mama stands fixing her hat to her gray hair with a long jet-tipped pin.

"You're too late for a hot breakfast," she warns me off further delay.

I have to bend to kiss her powdered and rouged cheek. She's heavy in the upper arms and calves but has a thin face. People say Mama let herself go after Marcella was born, as if it was a decision she made. Today she's wearing her good magenta dress, not new but not homemade and therefore sure to be noticed in the country. Her rimless glasses have flecks of flour on the lenses. She's dabbed lily of the valley behind her ears.

Mama passes me an old pair of scissors. She's in a hurry.

The roses for which she believes herself known grow on tangled bushes in the side-yard. Nobody has sprayed them and the petals are bug-eaten around the edges, but they are occasionally beautiful. This morning they've somehow retained dew despite the growing heat, and their fragrance hangs thick in the air.

I step over the little metal fence, hinged in sections, that marks the limits of the garden's domain and cut two bunches, reds and American Beauties. For no reason I twist a Heart's Delight into the top buttonhole of my dress. I could easily pass the day right here.

When I was a girl, the highlight of my year used to be going every summer with Papa to visit Grandma and Grandpa on the farm in Thebes. Now Mama, Marcella, and I make a pilgrimage the end of each May to pay respects and look into our future. With no dead husband to draw me to a foreign plot, I'll lay beside Mama and Papa, marked forever as a daughter who lived a long time. Marcella won't be there. In death she'll join Earl in Missouri.

I ignore the sound of the car horn until the third blast.

T HIS CAR SMELLS LIKE A FUNERAL parlor," observes Mama, pleased with her bounty. She's settled in her place, next to the passenger window in the front. Newspaper-wrapped roses are held steady between her broad knees. Marcella leans from the backseat, her arms crossed between Mama's and my shoulders.

"How you talk," she says. "Open the vent, Edna."

Marcella uses phrases from the car's instruction booklet, which she has read often. She's in awe of the Oldsmobile's technology and has faith that the vent can solve any problem, from heating to cooling to saving gas.

"I promised Dora eleven," insists Mama, "and it's pretty near ten now."

"Put it in the overdrive," suggests Marcella.

Market Street is quiet for the holiday. In the close Louisville morning heat, porch flags drape like wet towels. Nobody says anything as we drive past the house where we lived when Papa was alive and working, but each of us looks closely to see if it's been kept up.

"I like that off-white," says Marcella. "It's cheerful."

"Siding," Mama pronounces.

"Oh, no," objects Marcella. "It's too natural."

DORA QUICK IS PAPA'S SISTER-IN-LAW, our aunt by marriage. She has lived alone in the family house for seven years since Grandpa died at age one hundred. Directly next door is the new tiny branch of the First Thebes Savings and Loan. It's been recently rumored that the property is about to be demolished to make space for a parking lot, but today, resting in sagging, shabby contrast to the glass box of the bank, it's exactly as I remember. An azalea bush in the back partially conceals the weathered privy.

Dora has been on the lookout behind her curtains and is on the porch to greet us before we open the car door. She's a bone-thin woman with yellowed hair pulled into a coiled nest on the crown of her head. She wears, as ever, a print dress with a detachable filigree collar and worn-in black lace-shoes, tied secure in double bows. Her eyes, famous as her best feature for their piercing darkness, are hard and preoccupied behind violet-tinted bifocals.

"Here you are, here you are," she greets us. "Hot today, ain't it? Come in and take a load off. Nola and Herman'll be by so we can all go up together. Can you mount these steps, Allie? You're dressed fit to kill. Edna, you don't have one of your headaches, I pray? Marcella, you must be worn out after that long drive."

Mama bristles at being called Allie. Since moving to the city forty years ago she has been firmly "Mary Alice." None of the Thebes kin acknowledge her change, though now and then they do allow Papa to go from Bill to William out of respect for his passing and to make room for other Bills.

The parlor is chilly and dim, a shock after the blaze of daylight, and smells musty, like an old, rarely opened

268

clothes trunk. Family photographs of all types and from every period are taped to the walls and set on tables in frames. Sprung coils and springs make odd lumps in the settee. Cotton doilies decorate the tops of high-back chairs and cover the center of every flat-surfaced piece of furniture. Their creamy gatherings of thread and string are intricate as cobwebs.

Mama settles into a rocker, but Marcella and I stand. We don't want to remain in this cramped, crowded room for more than a few minutes. All of us dutifully follow Dora's gaze toward an iced angel food cake that rests on a sideboard.

"You all don't want to spoil your appetites," she tells us. "Of course I could cut you a slice now to tide you over."

Mama fans herself with her hand and shakes her head, satisfied that the offer has been made. I walk around looking at the pictures, passing among wedding parties and smiling cousins. I stop at the daguerreotypes, backed in molded metal and half-obscured behind a display of stiff-looking young men in World War II army uniforms.

"Is this Uncle Hector, Aunt Dora?" I say, lifting a tintype to study more closely.

"No. But he's a Quick of some kind. George, I think. Maybe Billy. My Hector never wore his hair in a center part."

"William wouldn't be caught dead in a hayseed suit like that," says Mama. She's raring for an argument, but I don't give her the chance.

"And this one?" I ask Dora. "She's kind of unusual."

"Sadie Yenawine. She was a gypsy. Or a Jewess. Russian. They say she came from Indianapolis to stay with Tommy Buck and never church-married him either. A regular scandal. We'll be going by their resting place today."

"Could you hunt us a cool drink, Dora?" asks Mama pointedly.

"Not for me. I need to observe the facilities." I walk through the kitchen, giving the pump handle a push. The slope-roofed outhouse still has its seat with two holes.

"Which is for which?" I'd joke when we were children, and Marcella would laugh like no tomorrow. She thought I made the moon.

Bees and mosquitoes fly in and out the ventilation window, cut in the shape of a five-point star. Looking through it, I see a car stop in front of the house.

B Y THE TIME I COME BACK INSIDE, Nola and her pale, sickly husband Herman are squeezed together on the hide-a-bed. As always, Nola has brought along a huge plastic bag stuffed with her awful homemade quilts. While she talks she smoothes one of them, a particular eyesore, across her lap.

"And Mother," she says to Dora, with a nod of greeting toward me, "he said he'd *never* seen so lovely a wedding band design—and he's traveled all over Indiana *and* Kentucky. He pronounced it so original he wanted to pay me seventy-five, on the spot, but I told him my relations from the city were traveling here today and I'd best offer it to them first—well, sit down, Edna—so it could rest in the family, you know? I said it would be a terrible shame to lose an heirloom forever, to just give it away to a stranger. Of course Herman here says I mustn't charge you folks any more than fifty—and I won't, but it's grand larceny at that price. I can see it on that nice cherry bed of Uncle Bill's, Aunt Allie."

A sigh passes over the room. Nola's henna hair is cut off-center, and she wears three costume bracelets on each wrist. Her rayon dress draws across her thighs as she leans forward from her seat. Every year we must escape a hard sell without hurting her feelings. Mama and Marcella look to me to save them.

"Nola, you do such fine stitch work but I had my heart set on . . ." I quickly scan what can be seen of the other quilts in the bag and name a design I don't see. "We were hoping for a *crazy* this year."

I'm risking plenty. Nola's crazies are head-spinning in their madness. Even to gaze at one, with its crooked hems and ill-matched pieces, can unhinge the brain.

"Don't that beat all?" Nola slams her open palm onto the quilt she holds. "I *told* Herman I should have brought the orange and green. But oh, no. He said . . . well, anyway, he said, 'They'd likely go for the wedding band,' and it *did* seem to me that you asked for a wedding band last year. How about one of these pretty Bethlehems?"

She bends over further, pulling an assortment from her bag, and strews them out in a half-circle around her feet. All are the same design, a sunburst of contrasting sateen diamonds sewn in the shape of the Magi's star onto squares of pre-quilted polyester.

"This here's 'coral' and this is 'citrus' and this one's 'midnight' something. A complement for every color scheme."

Marcella is all deadpan. "They are grand," she allows, "but Miss Edna did have her heart set on a crazy."

Mama has run out of patience. "You'd think you'd figure out, Nola, that bolt ends and remnants—"

"Mama," Marcella hurries in, "we ought to scoot. Edna, you warm the motor."

272

Herman follows cautiously with Dora and Mama together in the backseat of his rusty DeSoto. Nola, Marcella, and I ride the Olds in silence past familiar scenery, and in five minutes we turn into Our Lady of Peace. Along the lanes, winding cars are pulled off to the side and people, mostly elderly, weave through the tombstones looking for departed relatives and friends. They drift softly as leaves, collecting and dispersing. I ease into a space down the hill from Papa's plot and Herman parks behind.

We climb the path, bounded by limestone edgework, carrying food, quilts, flowers, vases, and pitchers. The large granite marker has a smooth rectangle already carved with Mama's name and "October 13, 1881–" Below it, there's an uninscribed blank reserved for me.

"Run on over to the well, Edna." Mama hands me the water jug. "Marcella will help me get the lunch laid out."

I pick my way past Johnsons and Williamses and Carters and Bucks to the flat, concrete-topped well, unhook the aluminum lard can that's kept there as a bucket, and lower it into the dark hole. It hits the water, tilts, and I retrieve it carefully, turning the rope around the pulley. It takes three good dippings to top the jug.

The mix of conversation, laughter, and insects swirls around me. Across the way, Mama pulls weeds at the base of Papa's headstone, Marcella oohs and aahs as Nola produces quilt after hideous quilt and flaps them for display. Dora has spread an extra checkered tablecloth on the ground and is in the slow process of arranging herself in its center. Herman works at his gums with a toothpick and looks out of place. He's always unsure whether to sit or stand on the graves of his wife's people.

I take my time returning. Dora and Mama are in their element. Watching each other closely, they divide the store of flowers into little bouquets and deposit each bunch into a glass jar or plastic vase ready to be disbursed among relatives buried around the graveyard.

"We'll give this one to Uncle William, that one to Miss Eliza," directs Mama with conviction.

"No, Allie. *This* one's Eliza's. She was closer to the Quicks than she was to your folks, and she always did favor my peonies."

"Dora, that woman was as attached to my mother as a sister, and I *think* I can spare her a rose. And anyway, I'm as much Quick as you are."

"Hector was the elder of the brothers, Bill was the younger," Dora points out, but she compromises and fits one of Mama's American Beauties into her arrangement.

Eventually the flowers are parceled and set in water, with the leftover from my jug poured into a pitcher. Nola squeezes the lemons and measures sugar for lemonade, and Marcella hands out paper plates laden with chicken, potato salad, bread and butter. Our coconut cake and Dora's guarded angel food will come later. By established custom, Mama and Dora will eat and flatter only the other's confection, but Marcella, Nola, Herman, and I must ask for a half-slice of each to show no preference.

"Your papa loved his chicken." Mama reaches in tribute for another breast. "He could put away four drumsticks before you could say 'Jack Robinson.'"

"That goes back to how they were raised," sniffs Dora. "Monnie spoiled her boys, never asked them for a lick of industry."

A flush spreads across Marcella's neck. "Papa worked like a Trojan," she says. "When he was down in Alabama for the railroad he put in twelve hours a day."

I glance at my sister. She likes to describe herself as a pacifist and rarely contradicts an opinion.

Dora brushes aside the objection. "I'm not saying they *couldn't* work when no woman was around to do for them. The two things Monnie loved: her bingo and her boys. Didn't give a hoot about anything or anybody else."

"Mama," Nola whispers loudly. "She lies right over yonder."

"It's nothing I didn't say to her poor old face a hundred times. That woman ruined herself and what did she have to show? Dead before her time and left me with the care of her invalid husband."

"Just because Hector never amounted to much don't mean William was lazy," says Mama. "And if I recall, Monnie *also* left you and Hector the house you live in."

Marcella stands and brushes off her dress. "Mama, walk me over to that Sadie?"

Mama sighs and rises slowly and in stages, first balancing on her hands and knees and then pulling herself erect with Papa's headstone as support. She tarries there a moment longer than necessary, smoothing the worn granite with the palm of one hand.

Finally, they abandon me, Nola, and Herman to listen to Dora's excuses for Hector. I nod in sympathy to everything she says. In my mind's eye, I can barely reconstruct the man's appearance.

HERMAN SITS ON THELMA CARTER'S stone and slips a plug of tobacco beneath his lower lip. "Them Masonic designs are right pretty, ain't they,

Nola?" he offers. "But I fail to decipher their meaning."

"Well, the Masonics ain't likely to reveal their secrets to you," Nola replies. "If you had let me bring that cute crazy, we could be on Easy Street this minute. Don't you *dare* spit in this churchyard."

Herman swallows, then gets to his feet and begins to repack the cars, glad for something to do.

Dora stacks the picnic plates like china before putting them into a brown trash bag, and hums softly.

"Is that a hymn, Aunt Dora?"

"Just some old tune Hector admired," she tells me. "Soon as I finish here I'm going to pin up this hair and go visit with him. He always prided me to be fixy. I don't suppose he minds that I ate over here with Bill and you all?"

I look at her, wondering if she's serious, but she only stares back, her garnet eyes insisting on my reassurance.

"I'm sure he'll understand when you explain the circumstances," I say, then feel ashamed of myself when she nods in appreciation.

"It don't seem reasonable he's gone seventeen years."

IN A LITTLE WHILE MARCELLA RE-turns, leaving Mama in the company of some distant kinfolks whose ties to us must be unscrambled. My sister and I are unaccustomed to being alone without a television or dishes to wash. Simple silence is embarrassing.

"Let's locate that old St. John's graveyard," Marcella suggests. "I haven't been over there in a good ten years, long before Earl was killed. It can't be much more than a mile beyond that rise."

"Does it bother you, being here?" I ask as we walk through the uncut brush at the woods' edge.

"You mean Earl? Not especially. It might be different if we'd been lucky and had a child, somebody to keep him alive for."

"Marcella!"

"I can't help it." She shifts her shoulders. "Earl's at rest. Back in this place, it's like I never left home, like I'm still single. It is the prettiest spot."

I don't jump to agree with her, so she steps within my silence.

"Why? Are *you* bothered?"

I realize, when she brings it up, that I am. The space that stands between me and my plot on the hill seems no time at all.

"I was remembering the first year Earl came over here with us," I say.

"He thought we were insane. He claimed people out west would never dream of picnics in the cemetery. He said it was a barbaric custom."

"Well, it won't persist for much longer." I find myself irritated with Earl and his opinions. "The average age of the living visitors today must be sixty-five. Nobody's likely to eat fried chicken on my tomb."

I'm interested that this idea comes as some relief.

"It's bad luck to talk like that!" Marcella warns. "You're young."

We're walking down a path of tire ruts overgrown with Queen Anne's lace. It crosses an open meadow that feels as quiet and big as the moon. Our voices are low but they carry through the air like the calls of birds. Living in the same house, my sister and I never talk about anything substantial. I share this thought.

"We know what each other is going to say before we say it, so we can save our breath." Marcella laughs at her own words, then walks for a moment in silence, stooping now and then to pick daisies in the high grass. "I could work out whole conversations with you in my mind," she continues.

"What would I say?"

Marcella glances at me. I make her nervous.

"You're in a mood today." She stops, holds her body stiff, and stares into the distance, then points across the swaying hay to a blackened frame just visible on the north horizon. "That's it. St. John's." We turn right and follow a line of grass that's grown a paler green than what sways on either side. It leads to our destination.

We stand in an overgrowth of thornbushes and wild alfalfa, on ground where the dead have forgotten the living. In another generation all signs that this clearing existed will have passed. It is the calmest place on earth. Only the slide of wind and the crush of our footsteps disturb the quiet.

"It's all going to seed," says Marcella. "Why don't they tend it?"

"There is no 'they' anymore. The pharaohs had the wisdom to build memorials of stone."

"There's no treasure in these pyramids, that's so." Marcella crosses her arms and meanders among the fallen headstones. "Just old feuds and fusses."

The sun is hot and my legs are tired. I rest against a piece of limestone, jutting from the earth, and tug at a tough stem of weed. There's a prick upon the skin of my breast. I have forgotten the rose in my buttonhole and feel foolish that I've worn it through the day. I take it out, roll the velvet petals between my thumb and fingers, then drop it to the ground.

"Do I ever argue with you in those conversations inside your head?" I ask Marcella.

"Will you stop?" She changes the subject. "I can't get Papa off my brain. Do you still miss him as much as you did?"

"Not as much."

It isn't true. There are things I still wonder about him, questions I'd like to know his answers to, stories he never finished telling me. "You were so little when he died. Just eight. He must be a blur in your memory."

"Well . . ." Marcella looks off across the meadow.

"Well," she starts again, "it's funny, but I was forever comparing Earl to Papa. Isn't that something? It wasn't that I remembered so many facts, exactly, I just had this kind of impression. Earl never measured up to it."

Marcella hears herself and covers her mouth with her hand. "Will you listen to me? Earl was a decent provider. He was an expert ballroom dancer."

"Earl was all right," I agree. "But you're right, I don't see much of Papa in him."

Marcella opens her mouth, yet instead of answering she rips some clematis away from a bleached, thin stone marker that slants into the ground at her feet.

"I love these things." She reads aloud: " 'James Lee Quick. Born 1841 in Thebes, Indiana. Died, a Hero,

1862 in Murfreesboro, Tennessee. Preserve The Union.' And 'Elizabeth May Manion. Born 1838 in Thebes, Indiana. Betrothed of J. L. Quick. Pined Away 1863.' Twenty-five, what a waste. What would they term 'pining away' these days? Cancer? Pneumonia?"

"The loss of the will to live." I move beside her, trace my index finger over the stone. "She had nothing to do but die."

Marcella puts her hands on her hips, strikes a pose.

"You romantic! I was wrong about what I said: I can't predict you. That's twice today."

"I can't predict myself."

"Sometimes, Edna, you can be so *different,* just like Papa. I try and recollect him and it gets confused with things about you. I see him in you more and more as we get older."

I reach for Marcella's hand. Even in the heat of the afternoon, her skin is cool to the touch, dry.

"Earl was jealous, did you know that?" she suddenly whispers. "He said all I wanted was to bask in your shadow."

I see my sister as she was. Running hard to catch me. Shaping finger waves on her forehead. Graduating high. Leaving home to marry Earl at his army post. Coming back from his funeral a lost soul. I have this swell of feeling for her, but there is no channel between us, no unshuttered window.

"It's only nine years that divides us," I say. "Nine years is nothing when you're grown."

I wait for her to look at me, but she stands frozen, her skirt shifting in the breeze. Her grip has no strength. Her arm is like a curtain held back by the sash of my hand. I let it go.

"Your hair looks so nice, Marcella," I say at last. "Did you put something on it?"

Grateful, she touches her bangs. "I don't know. I did try a new perm."

Mama is sitting in the back-seat of the Oldsmobile, waiting to leave.

"It's going to be bumper to bumper," she forecasts ominously as Marcella and I get in the front.

Herman, Nola, and Dora have already departed. We will catch them at Grandpa's house to say good-bye.

"Don't it look nice, though?" Mama observes. The green cemetery lawn is dotted with florals and the small American flags placed before a few headstones.

Marcella rolls down her window, adjusts the sideview mirror, and applies fresh lipstick. "Mama . . ." she begins, then blots her lips on a tissue. "Did you ever think Papa and my Earl were much alike?"

"Two peas from the same pod," Mama answers behind me.

I twist in my seat to stare at her, amazed. "They weren't a whit the same." I turn to Marcella. "Not a whit."

Herman and Nola have stopped by their house and are set to return any minute.

"Don't be in a hurry," Dora tells us. There's a tremble to her voice. Tears ride in her eyelids, and she makes no effort to wipe them away—they are there to be seen. "This may be *it.*"

Nola rushes in from outside, breathless, but halts at the sight of her mother.

"What's wrong?" she cries. Herman, startled by his wife's voice, lets the screen door slam behind him.

"Dora Quick, you will dance on all our graves!" says Mama. "You just crave attention."

"Aunt Allie! You take that back." Nola swings toward Mama, but Dora won't be interrupted.

"Alice Marie . . ." she begins, then fans herself with a page of creased paper, widens her blackbird eyes. "Now I'll have to join the angels to prove you wrong!"

"You get Nola to bring you to town this summer," Mama says. She dabs behind the corners of her glasses with a napkin.

A look I cannot read passes between them, joins them like memory.

"Mama, the holiday traffic," Marcella breaks in. "Edna's exhausted."

They all turn to see. I close my eyes and open them. The long row of photographs faces me across the dim room.

"Before you go!" Nola still blocks the doorway. "I found that crazy. It's right here, ready to be stretched over a double bed."

She clutches a wild rash of green and orange cloth, bunched as if dragged from the back of a closet or the far corner of an attic. It catches the afternoon light passing through thin curtains and glows like a ball of fire.

"Twenty dollars, Nola. Take it or leave it."

She's too stunned and suspicious to reply, and stands holding the polyester bundle tight as a baby in her arms. Mama stares at me as though I've lost my mind.

"She'll take it!" Herman says, coming to life and snatching the quilt from Nola's grasp. He thrusts it forward. "Cash on delivery."

"It's a present for Marcella." My voice is high, but under control.

I dig into my purse for the money and ignore my sister's eyes.

"Edna, what are you thinking! You're more than

generous, but I couldn't possibly accept! It'd be perfect for *your* room."

"We can *dye* it . . ." Mama starts, before she sees my face.

"I can decorate around it." Marcella's tone is uncertain. She doesn't understand the joke and fears that she has said a wrong thing.

I accept the quilt from Herman, shake it out once to full glory, then fold it into tight, ordered squares. In my hands, it's weightless as air.